THE ADVENTURES OF PHILIP AND SOPHIE

The Sword of the Dragon King: Part I

DREW ELDRIDGE

Email: theadventuresofphilipandsophie@gmail.com

ISBN 978-1-7781088-1-5

For my Students

"May it be a light for you in dark places,
when all other lights go out."
— J.R.R. Tolkien

CONTENTS

PROLOGUE
THE ARGUMENT

Every morning, when the sun rose and a gentle breeze brought up the scent of lilies, a little bird named Sebastian Ploomberry would wake up, shake out his little feathers, stretch his little legs, and peer down over the edge of his little nest. He had been practicing all summer for what was to be the most exciting moment of his life: the moment when, for the very first time, he would get to spread out his wings and fly.

"Alright," he repeated to himself confidently. "Just like we rehearsed. Feet tucked . . . back straight . . . beak pointed to where I want to go . . . and wings up-down, up-down!"

As Sebastian said this, he hopped up onto the ledge and began readying himself by pacing back and forth and taking a series of deep little breaths.

"Oh bother! Why does it have to be so high up?" he exclaimed. "I shall surely break my head if I fall! Then what would become of me?"

The sun seemed much brighter to Sebastian suddenly, and the wind felt much stronger. If any other little bird had been in his place, they would have more than likely gotten scared and turned back. But Sebastian was different from most other little birds—braver and more curious. For better or worse, he was very often able to talk himself into such things, even if it got him into trouble.

"No! No! No!" he shouted out. "I'm not going to chicken out again! Not *this* time! Not *this* bird! I'm going over, and that's all there is to it!"

Sebastian then took a *very* deep breath (a breath so deep, in fact, that it made him look like he was about to burst or blow up into a puff of feathers), bent his knees, and began to count down backwards from three.

"If I do that," he thought to himself, "then, perhaps it will be like someone is here with me cheering me on . . . Three! Two! One!" he counted. But it didn't work. It was still too scary! He couldn't move and felt very disappointed in himself. "Oh, dear . . ." he sighed.

But then Sebastian had another idea. One he was sure would work!

"Oh! Oh! I know! Perhaps if I close my eyes as I count . . . Yes, that should do it!" he thought. "You can't get scared if you can't see!" Once more, he started counting. "Three, two and one!" But the same thing happened again. What was he going to do? He was out of ideas.

"Oh well," he lamented, "I'll just have to do it the old-fashioned way, I guess. No tricks! No funny business!" He cleared his throat and prepared himself one last time. "Ahem, ahem! Wings, don't fail me!" he cried out to the heavens. "Wind, lift me up! And . . . as for the rest of the world . . ." Sebastian was hurrying now because he realized he was stalling again. "Here . . . I . . . come!"

And with that, Sebastian yelled out the word "Go!" as loud as he could—and plunged himself forward with all his might! A cold gust of wind then burst up from under him and thrust his whole body into the air! He lost his balance for a moment, and the sun's bright beams nearly blinded him, but he managed to straighten himself out.

"I'm doing it!" he exclaimed, flapping his little wings. "I'm flying! I'm really flying! How delightful! How wonderful! How—"

But before Sebastian could finish what he was going to say, he felt a firm clamp upon the tip of his little tail and a strong tug backward

—pulling him, in fact, right straight back to the place where he began. It was his older sister.

"Ouch! What was that for?" Sebastian whimpered, as he landed on his back with a thud.

"For your own good, that's what!" his sister replied. "Just where do you think you were going?"

"I was *going* to fly," said Sebastian, "until *you* interrupted me. It's boring here! There's nothing to do!"

Sebastian spoke as though he had been awakened from the most wonderful dream he had ever had, and was now being jostled out of bed. He stood up and began brushing himself off very grumpily.

"What do you mean there's nothing to do?" said his sister. "I play with you, don't I?"

"Yes, yes, but you're a girl! All girls ever want to do is play 'nest' or sing! And Edward is always out helping mother." Sebastian huffed. "Well, I for one have seen enough of nests for now. It's high time I discover something new!"

The place Sebastian was referring to, and which he kept pointing at with his wing as he spoke, was the great green forest beyond the Ploomberry nest—a valley that was very old, very mysterious, and full of many wondrous spectacles. Every day, Sebastian would imagine himself exploring them.

"First," he would say to himself, as he held out his wing and squinted, "to the great snowy mountain to the East! And then to the rushing rivers! And then—" if that wasn't enough, and if he "had time," as he always added, "—to one of the many tall roaring waterfalls with rainbows over them!"

Sebastian's nest was in the Life Tree. It was the tallest of all the trees in the great valley, and was right in the middle. That meant he had the best view. In every direction, there was something wonderful to look at! He used to day-dream about what might be there. Sebastian saw adventure! Excitement! But all Dorabella saw was trouble.

"You're too little," she continued in that tone that big sisters so love to lecture their little brothers in. "Your wings aren't long enough. Your beak is too short. And you don't even—"

"Ah, fooey!" said Sebastian. "I would have made it . . ."

"Made it where, Sebastian? I still don't understand. What is it you want to do down there, anyway?"

He didn't even have to think about it.

"Why, go on an adventure, of course! Just like—"

But then Sebastian was interrupted again, this time by his older brother bird, who had just flown down and landed behind him.

"Oh, don't tell me he's prattling on about that old peacock's tale again," the voice sneered. "Really, Dorabella, you should not be encouraging him."

Now, as you know, reader, you should never, ever try to hit one of your brothers or sisters, even when they say something mean you don't like. It's always better to use words to solve problems, or to call a grown up and let them sort it out. I'm very sorry to say, however, that young Sebastian did not do this. Instead, he lost his temper and charged forth towards his brother with an intent on dealing a most severe pecking! And his brother, too, did the same! Fortunately, their sister managed to get between them just in time.

"Now enough of that, you two! I said enough!"

"He started it!" cried Sebastian.

"I don't care who started it," Dorabella responded. "And you, Edward, stop behaving like such a child!"

"I'm only trying to teach the kid a lesson! The sooner he grows up and faces the truth, the better."

Sebastian then scowled at his brother and stuck his tongue out. So did Edward.

"Stop it!" Dorabella got between them. "I'll tell mother! I will!" They stopped immediately. "What in the world are you two arguing about, anyways?"

"Nothing," grumbled Edward.

Sebastian clearly disagreed.

"It's *not* nothing!" he corrected. "The whole forest is talking about it, sis! Something extraordinary has happened!"

"What's happened?" she asked.

"There's a *new* creature! A powerful one! Who fights on OUR side!"

THE MYSTERIOUS CREATURE

The forest was divided into the strong and the weak—and the weak were always preyed upon by the strong. That's why the news was so hard for everyone to believe. But the news was spreading fast! All the little chicks were chirping about it:

There is a creature,
Big and strong,
Chirp, chirp!
Who was once very naughty,
and did much wrong.
Chirp! Chirp!
Until one day,
The creature switched sides.
Chirp!
Now our protector,
Guardian of nests, trees and hives . . .

"The Legend of the Seven Labors" was what the chicks were all calling it—"seven" being the number of evil king-animals the creature had de-throned. Sebastian Ploomberry was one of these little chicks. He had memorized every riddle and song about the creature and hoped one day to join him. Either that, or become a hero himself and have his own adventures. But his brother didn't believe it was really true and his sister was only learning about the legend for the first time. If he could only convince her, then maybe she would let him go. In his best storyteller's voice, he began reciting the tale.

"He wanders around, they say . . . getting into adventures! Rescuing . . . fighting battles . . . chasing villains . . ." As he spoke, he sawed through the air with his wing like a sword, making swish sounds: "taking from the rich . . . giving to the poor . . . and protecting the weak from the powerful!"

But Edward wasn't about to let him get away with it. He thought the story was silly.

"And who has hands, but no claws . . ." he interrupted sarcastically. "Skin, but no fur or feathers . . . And who can go invisible, weave spider webs, and fly without having any wings! Right!?"

Edward crossed his arms and rolled his eyes.

"That's right!" answered Sebastian confidently. "Except about the fur part. It does have fur, so I've heard—only it's all on the top of its head, rather than its body—"

"Oh, how convenient!" harped back Edward. He was so annoying. "Of course! Its fur is all on its head! How silly of me! By my beak—the next thing you'll be telling us is that this creature who wanders about doesn't even have a tail!"

"Actually," replied Sebastian, closing his eyes and pointing upward, "that is the next thing I was about to mention . . ."

Edward finally snapped. You could tell, because all his feathers began to stand up like a porcupine. He didn't like it when Sebastian told these kinds of stories. He thought they were dangerous. They made impressionable little birds want to go on adventures—which was a very good way of getting eaten up.

"That's it!" Edward cried out, flapping his wings. "I have heard enough of this nonsense, Sebastian! There is no such creature! And there will be no more talk of it! Or of any other silly myth you've made up! And that's that!"

But Sebastian would not be silenced. It was too important to him.

"You believe me, don't you, sis?" Sebastian asked as he hopped over and began tugging on her wing.

But Dorabella still wasn't sure.

"I don't know, Sebastian," she replied. "It does sound awfully far-fetched . . ."

She believed it was a dangerous idea too.

"And no adventures either!" Edward added with a scoff. "I'm the oldest! I know best! And I say that's the new rule! You only want to go on one, anyways, because you are young! *You* don't know what it was like before we built this place! How hard life was! How much was lost!"

Sebastian hated it when people brought up his age in a bad way—as if everything he said was automatically wrong merely because of his small stature. Besides, what was wrong with adventures? They were dangerous? So what? He didn't care. It was a lot better, in his opinion, than sitting around in a boring old nest or looking for worms all day. But Edward clearly didn't get it.

"And you don't know what it's like," Sebastian fired back angrily, "not to know what it was like! Being cooped up all day, where nothing important or exciting ever happens! And never having anything interesting to say to anyone, apart from about what others have done or what we only get to watch going on down below. You had an adventure helping find the Life Tree. Why can't I have one of my own? And why can't it be even grander!?"

They were both so loud that many of the other birds from the other nests were beginning to listen in, too.

"I want to have my own story," Sebastian continued, "to be remembered for doing something!"

"We are doing something," said Edward, grumpily. "We're surviving! Trust me when I say that's as good as it gets."

"Ah, fooey!" said Sebastian again, this time with a pout. "That's all you ever say! But you don't know that. You don't know anything!"

"I know that if you leave, you'll die," said Edward sternly. "How would you like to be remembered for that, little brother? And for your sister's death, too, when she comes to rescue you? Or, while you're at it, why not drag the whole nest down with you? That would be an interesting story!"

Sebastian was now fuming. If you could have seen beneath his feathers, he would have been a bright hot red color. And if he had had fists, they would have been clenched with fury.

"I never said anyone had to come after me!"

"But they will. You do know that, don't you?"

"Well . . . that's their problem then! Either way, it would be a lot better than staying here! I hate this place!" he growled. "And I hate both of you!"

A quiet sadness fell over all who were listening in the tree—especially Dorabella—and Sebastian immediately regretted saying that.

"Oh great . . . great . . ." he thought to himself, feeling perfectly rotten. "Now look what I've done! Me and my big beak!"

He crossed his wings and huffed as everyone looked at him with disappointment. Sebastian knew he had to apologize. Nevertheless, he still didn't feel like Edward, Dorabella or anyone else understood him. And it was very frustrating. Now that he had everyone's attention, maybe he could finally explain.

"Listen," he continued. "I'm sorry for what I said. I didn't mean that. I was just angry, that's all. I do like it here. Of course, I do! It's my home. But all I am simply stating is that . . . well . . ." Sebastian hopped up onto the ledge and pointed to the great valley again. "Maybe there is more out there for us! You know? That . . . maybe building a nest and being safe is only a part of life—or a first step to something bigger!"

All of the birds in the tree looked at each other confused. Something more? Bigger? What in the world was Sebastian talking about?

"You mean . . . like a bigger nest?" Dorabella asked curiously.

"Maybe," Sebastian answered. "Sure!"

It wasn't exactly what he himself had in mind—but hey, at least it was something. At least they were thinking about it. Dorabella suddenly seemed interested. All of the birds did. They each spent a moment or two pondering it. Even Edward. Maybe Sebastian was right. Maybe there was more to life for a bird. And maybe there really was a hero creature. Sebastian smiled. Finally, he felt like he'd gotten through to them. But then something happened.

"Well, we shall know soon enough," said Edward. "If you are right, Sebastian, then I suppose we're in for quite the show this morning . . ."

"What do you mean?" answered Sebastian. "A show? What kind of show?" And what did it have to do with adventures or the mysterious creature? Dorabella was wondering too. Everyone was.

"What kind do you think?" answered Edward. "It's why I've flown back so early. I was going to tell you right away, but you kept arguing with me. The Black Beard Gang is headed this way."

"What? What did you just say!?" Sebastian

yelled, panicking. "The Black Beards are coming? That's what you've been waiting to tell us this whole time? Are you crazy!?"

The Black Beards, reader, were a gang of some of the most mean and nasty apes in the whole forest. They stole, bullied, kidnapped and sometimes even killed other animals for fun! They hadn't been seen in the Life Tree for several months, and the birds there were just beginning to feel safe again. But now it seemed like everyone's worst nightmares had come true. As you would expect, the whole place broke into a panic.

"Coo! Coo!" the doves sang, frantically. "The apes are back! The apes are back! What are we going to doOoOoOo!"

"Chip, chip! Chip, chip! Chip, chip!" said the squirrels.

And all the little chipmunks began hoarding as many acorns in their cheeks as they could before hiding. Sebastian was speechless.

"Quiet, please!" called out Edward, trying to calm everyone down. "Chirping about it is not going to help!"

Poor Dorabella looked more worried than anyone. She was barely able to speak without trembling.

"Are you sure you saw them?" she squeaked

timidly. "Are you sure it was the Black Beard Gang?"

"Positive," said Edward.

"How many?"

"That depends if you include the captives . . ."

"They have captives!?" Sebastian shouted.

"Three," replied Edward, "of the Brumble-dumb family."

The Brumbledumbs were another group of apes who lived in the forest—who the Black Beard Gang often picked on for being weaker. By the sounds of it, the Black Beard Gang had just finished raiding the Brumbledumbs' home and were now returning to the Life Tree to celebrate.

"But how many of the gang are coming?" Dorabella exclaimed.

Neither of the two brothers had ever seen their sister so distraught before.

"What does it matter how many?" replied Edward. "There's a hero who's going to save us all! Right, Sebastian?"

But Sebastian didn't seem very sure anymore.

"Well, what's wrong?" Edward teased. Then he laughed at his little brother. And it was precisely this laughing that made Sebastian do what he did next. Amidst the panic, he hopped up onto a branch overhead. And then to another one!

"Oh, Sebastian!" Dorabella cried. "Where are you going?"

He hopped up on one more, until he was at the very top of the tree! Then he took a deep breath, flapped his wings and yelled as loud as he could so all could hear:

"Yes! He WILL come! You'll see!" All of the birds immediately stopped panicking and looked up at him. "I know you don't believe, Edward! But you're wrong! The mighty creature IS real! He WILL COME. He'll come—and he'll SAVE US ALL!"

The whole tree shook with cheers after Sebastian said this, much to Edward's annoyance. In fact, there was so much cheering that some of the nests even came close to tumbling right off their branches. Sebastian had to be very careful getting back down and nearly started fighting with his brother again. But it all came to an end when another even louder sound was suddenly heard. A familiar sound that all animals in the tree dreaded.

"Shh! Did you hear that?" cried Dorabella.

Everyone listened.

Boom . . .

Boom . . .

Boom . . .

"Ooh Ahh . . ."

"Ooh Ahh . . ."

"Ooh Ahh . . ."

Boom!

Boom!

"Ooh Ahh!"

"Ooh Ahh!"

The Black Beard Gang had returned . . .

2

THE BLACK BEARD GANG

When Sebastian, Dorabella and Edward heard the horrible Black Beard Gang approaching, they hopped over to the edge of their nest and peeked down quietly together.

"Do you think they'll find us?" whispered Dorabella.

"They've never found us before," said Edward. "But there is no guarantee they won't find us this time."

"I wish they would just leave us alone!" pouted Sebastian. "It's not fair that they pick on us. We don't bother them!"

"Of course, it's not fair, Sebastian," his sister lamented. "But that's the way life is in the forest. Some are strong and some are weak. Some get to eat and some get eaten. We just have to accept it and keep hiding."

Sebastian and Edward frowned. They didn't like hearing it, but the truth was their sister was right. In this forest, there was no justice. There were no police officer animals. There were no courts or judges. There was nothing at all—nothing but bullies competing to see who could be the cruelest. For whoever was cruelest was always the most feared in the forest. And whoever was most feared could always get their way. The leader of the Black Beard Gang, Old Black Beard himself, was just one of many who were trying to fight their way to the top.

"Out of'r way ye scoundrels!" some of them yelled as they swung into the great tree. "Ooh Ahh! Ooh Ahh!"

"Make way for the king of the forest!"

They did everything they could to make sure everyone was good and miserable, as bullies do. They kicked! They spat! They pushed other animals down! They shoved! They called names! They also made a very great mess of the great tree wherever they swung to—ripping off the bark or tearing branches for fun.

One little tree frog got the worst of it. An ape reached into its little house hole, dragged it out by its legs, spun it round and threw it so far and so high that it looked like it disappeared into the clouds! Fortunately for our little friend, however, it ended up falling down safely onto a lily-pad in a pond a short ways away.

"Monsters!" cried young Sebastian, as he watched helplessly. He imagined himself being much bigger and liked it. "Why, if only I were an eagle, I would swoop down and peck those big bullies' brains out! That would teach them! And then! Mmmm-mm-mm-mm-mm-mm!"

Sebastian was trying to say, "and then lift them up high and drop them," but couldn't because Dorabella had covered his mouth with her wing.

"Shh! They'll hear you!"

The family of birds, in what was once a cozy and safe nest, looked down together at the mayhem the tree was now in, searching and searching for the captives Edward had seen. And, sure enough, there they were on one of the branches, huddling and shivering together. But there was also something familiar about them. Sebastian squinted.

"Wait a minute!" He broke away from his sister's grasp. "That's Lumpy! And his friends! He often climbs up here and plays with me!"

"Sebastian Ploomberry!" said Dorabella. "You should not be playing with strange apes like that!"

"Lumpy's not strange," Sebastian replied. "He's kind! And SO funny!"

"It's true," spoke another softer voice coming from behind all three of the birds. They spun around and looked up—and there on a branch they saw a butterfly and a squirrel.

"The Brumbledumbs," said the butterfly, ever so softly, the way a butterfly would, "are a noble family who never try to hurt or steal from anyone. Your brother is perfectly safe around them. I assure you."

"That's right!" the squirrel added, in a squeakier and somewhat, I dare say, cheekier sounding voice. "Especially Lumpy!"

Edward was curious about why the butterfly and squirrel had come up so high.

"Are you two leaving the tree?" he asked.

"That's the plan," replied the squirrel with a chirp. "We're going to live down by the waterfall."

"You should come with us," said the butterfly, batting her eyelashes.

"The waterfall?" Dorabella answered. "But you can't live there!" She could hardly speak. "Th-th-th-that's where the t-t-tiger lives . . ."

But the butterfly and squirrel didn't even flinch.

"Not anymore," the squirrel responded.

"Word has it, the tiger has been . . . taken care of . . . and that the animals there now roam freely and safely!"

"Really?" Dorabella asked.

"Mmmhmm," both of them responded together.

Sebastian's feathers pricked up in excitement and he burst past his sister from behind her.

"Ah-hah!" he cried out. "Mysterious disappearances! I told you HE was real, Edward! I told you!"

Edward rolled his eyes.

"Ah, so you've heard about it too, I see," said the squirrel, scratching his chin.

"Heard about it?" said Edward. "It's all the kid ever chirps about! Hero this! And savior that! I really wish he'd just—"

Sebastian cut him off before he could finish.

"Did you see him!? What did he look like? No tail or fur, right!?"

"Mmm . . . no . . . I didn't see him," answered the squirrel. "But I do know someone who did once . . ."

"Do you think he'll come?"

The squirrel and the butterfly looked at each other and shrugged.

"I hope he does," said Sebastian. He looked back down over the edge at poor Lumpy, surrounded by all those mean apes. "I know he will! He must!"

Speaking of Lumpy, reader, he was having

quite the time down there as all this was happening. For Lumpy was not the sort of apeling who was captured so easily. One of the bad apes learned that when they tried to grab him and eat him up!

"How'd ye like to be my dinner! Yarrr!"

It reached out with its long arms and snagged Lumpy's ankle. It picked him up and brought him right up close to its big, ugly face, where you could smell its rotten breath.

"Yesss . . ." the beast croaked slowly, glaring at him. "Ye will be tasteyyy . . ."

Everyone who was watching thought Lumpy was a goner for sure—especially his two friends, who were each so scared they could hardly even stand. But Lumpy managed to struggle free!

"Ouch! Ouch! Ouch!" yelped his captor. "That little bugger bit me!"

Lumpy stuck his tongue out at him. But to get revenge, the big ape kicked him really hard, which sent Lumpy rolling like a little furry soccer ball, down the branch and crashing into the trunk of the tree. That was about when all the ruckus ended, and the evil ape king, Old Black Beard, called for everyone to stop. His voice was scary, but intelligent-sounding, rolling his r's and puffing up his chest, like he fancied himself to be some kind of royalty.

"Enough! There shall be no eating of the

spoils! These meddling rrr-rascals must suffah a different fate! Gather rrr-ound then, everrr-yone and listen to what I say!"

The Black Beard Gang did as they were told, and soon everyone was sitting around the ape king in a circle, as though they were in a theatre watching a play. The Life Tree was big enough to fit everyone. When the apes finally settled, Old Black Beard cleared his throat and continued, seeming to want to give a speech. Sebastian and the rest of the birds and animals listened in, wondering what he had planned.

"Ahem ahem . . . Brrr-others! Countrymen! Comrrr-ades!" he yelled. "Today has been a grrr-eat victory for The Black Beards! We have conquered the territory of the tortoises! Swept thrrr-ough the valley of the so-called vulture king! And have crrr-ushed all who have stood in our way! The forrr-est belongs to us now! Ooh Ahh! Ooh Ahh!"

Everyone but the good animals in the tree cheered and beat their chests.

"Ooh Ahh! Ooh Ahh! Ooh Ahh!"

Oh, the nerve they had in saying that, reader! It made all of the other animals feel so angry! They didn't belong to him! And neither did their homes! But, on the other hand, that was the rule . . . wasn't it? With no one around to stop them, the strongest got to do what they wanted. And if you tried to resist or complain or show any sign of rebellion . . . well, that usually meant death.

The king continued.

"But! Our work is not over, com-rrrades! No! For although we have achieved victory, there still rrr-emain some who rrr-esist us! Animals like the DUMB DUMB family!" Old Black Beard said the name wrongly like this on purpose, reader, just to annoy animals like Sebastian—and it worked. "Who grrr-eedily store up bananas, and try to hide them when it's time to share! Liars! Cheaters! Frauds! All of them! How dare they not share, comrades! Ooh Ahh! Ooh Ahh! How dare they not share!" More cheers followed before he continued. "Ahem! Which is why, comrades . . . we have captured some prrr-inces of the DUMB DUMB family! To make an example of them! So they never trrr-y it again! And to rrr-emind all of you other pathetic crrr-eatures listening what will happen to you, too . . . if you choose to rrr-esist us, as well! Ooh Ahh!"

The entire Black Beard Gang cheered for a third time, repeating the king like parrots and drumming on the branches. It could be heard for miles throughout the whole valley and made all of the weaker animals despair. There were many long faces and frowns in the Life Tree that day.

But then . . . another voice suddenly spoke up from the crowd of apes that didn't sound at all like the others. Far from being confident and bully-like, it was a voice that trembled in fear. It was something that none of the smaller animals had ever seen before.

"B-b-but!" it cried, quivering and shivering. "W-w-what about . . . the . . . the . . . Phantom Ape? I've heard i-i-it eats animals who hurt o-o-others like that . . ."

He looked over his shoulder, scared that something might be lurking behind him. Others in the gang began doing the same.

"Yes, I've heard that too!" you could hear some of them whisper.

"Isn't that what happened to Johnny?"

"I heard it breathes fire!"

"I heard it walks on water!"

"I heard it—"

And so on. It was clear, reader, that the ape king had completely lost control of his gang. He clenched his fists and growled in frustration. Only our young Sebastian seemed to know what everyone was suddenly so worried about.

"Phantom Ape?" he thought as he listened. "I wonder if that's the Black Beard Gang's name for . . . Yes, it must be!"

Old Black Beard snarled and sneered some more. Then, he shouted to get everyone's attention. It was the second time that week the mysterious creature had come up, and it was really beginning to get on his nerves.

"Enough! Silence! Order!" he growled while flinging about his arms. "Do not be fooled by these stories you have heard about phantom apes! They are all lies! Lies, I tell you! Do you hear me? 'Tis a myth! A legend! Common fables, made up by the weak crrr-eatures to make themselves feel better as we rule them! And that's all! Yes! The only ape anyone needs to be afrrr-aid of . . . is me! And today I shall prrr-ove it to you once and for all!"

There was a brief silence after that as the animals on both sides began to wonder what the old ape king might have meant. Prove it? How would he do that?

"Brrr-ing out the Stomper!"

"The Stomper?" whispered Dorabella to her brothers. "Who's that?"

Sebastian and Edward looked at each other equally as puzzled. They had no idea.

"Oh, I don't like the sound of this . . ." she whimpered.

Then, everyone heard a loud sound they recognized from before.

Boom . . .

Boom . . .

Boom . . .

"Ooh Ahh! Ooh Ahh!"

Boom!

Boom!

"Ooh Ahh! Ooh Ahh!"

What was that? An elephant? A hippopotamus? The birds and squirrels in the great tree were all confused. And why was it that now, after hearing that awful noise, the Black Beard Gang all started smiling and laughing again?

"Bah hah hah hah!"

"Ooh ooh! Ah ah!"

"Hoo hoo hee! This will be good!"

"Yes! The Stomper! Muah hah hah!"

And then they saw it, reader! The biggest, strongest, ugliest, stupidest-looking ape ever to walk in that wild valley, swinging through the branches toward them, with poor, poor little Lumpy straight in its path.

"By my tail! Do you see the size of that monster?" Sebastian yelled. "Lumpy! Look out! Run away! Hurry!"

"Oh, please hush, Sebastian!" whispered Dorabella. "You never can just be quiet, can you? Shh!"

When the beast landed onto the branch Lumpy and his friends were on, it felt like an earthquake. The whole tree shook and trembled. Lumpy sat like a toddler at the giant's feet, each of which were bigger than he was! The giant, Stomper, had a long beard, a round fat belly, with two legs as thick as the branch he was standing on. And all that drool! The foul creature looked down at Lumpy cross-eyed and laughed the stupidest-sounding laugh you ever heard—like this:

"Ho! Ho! Ho! . . . Hoo! Hoo! Hoo! . . . Ho! Ho! . . . Ho! Ho! . . . Me, Stomper! Me hungry. Me stomp on little apes and make food. Ooh Ahh! Ooh Ahh! Ho! Ho! Ho!"

You see what I mean?

"Who shall I stomp first? This one? That one? Or this little runt right here! Ho! Ho!"

Lumpy gulped again, for of the three captive apes "the littlest" was in fact him. And this time he was too scared to try and run away or fight.

"No matter," said the giant ape. "I can stomp all of 'em at once, they're so tiny . . . Ho! Ho! Ho! Ho!"

The king laughed together with Stomper. So did the rest of the gang. It made the birds, squirrels and everyone else feel like it was even more hopeless. Everyone, that is, except for Sebastian. Though, even he was beginning to have doubts now. He looked around frantically for any sign of the hero he believed in, but saw no one.

"Blast! Where is he!?"

Time was running out.

"Now," announced the evil king proudly. "Let this be a reminder to all of you weak cr-r-reatures!" He raised his hand, preparing to give Stomper the signal. "And a lesson for your children! And your children's children! About what happens when you step out of your place! And forget that your r-r-role in the forest is to serve animals like me! Bah, hah hah hah! Bah! Hah hah hah! Hah hah!"

The gang all laughed with him, and started mocking them more:

"Bah hah hah hah! Look at them all! Look how scared the little babies are! How pathetic!"

"Yeah! Crying for their mommies and daddies! Ooh, hoo hoo!"

"Or their make-believe hero! Looks like he's not coming!"

"Because he isn't real!"

"No one's coming!"

"Stomper's going to crush you!"

"Yeah! And make you even uglier!"

"Ooh Ahh! Ooh Ahh!"

"Oh ho! Look at their faces! What's wrong, babies? Aw, I think they're going to cry! Haw! Haw! Haw!"

And so on and so forth, reader. It was terrible! They sounded so stupid. Yet none of the good animals had anything at all they could say back, or do. What could they? Maybe Old Black Beard was right. Edward began to feel sorry for making fun of Sebastian. For deep down, he realized that he wanted there to be a hero, just like everyone else did. Stomper raised his foot and waited for the signal to stomp.

"It's a shame," Edward lamented. "I really liked Lumpy and his friends. I only wish I could have had the chance to say goodbye to them . . ." He let out a sad, sad sigh.

"Oh Lumpy," added Sebastian, about to break into tears. "I'm so sorry. Goodbye, my friend . . ."

Dorabella was so sad that she could hardly make a sound. All she could do was cover her eyes with her wings and squeak. "I can't watch!"

That just left Stomper, Lumpy and his friends. The little apes hugged each other— thinking it would be their last moment alive. The Black Beard Gang all beat their chests and pounded on the branches of the tree, like a drum roll: "Ooh Ahh! Ooh Ahh! Ooh Ahh!" Finally, the evil king dropped his hand, giving the signal to squash them!

"Ho, ho, ho . . ." laughed Stomper. "Ho! Ho! Ho!" His foot was up and over top of them! "HO! HO! HO!" But . . . he didn't end up stomping with it.

"Wait!" yelled Sebastian suddenly, at the top of his little lungs, throwing up his wings. He saw something! He saw something approaching! Moving really fast! And I mean, really fast! Swinging through the branches! It was getting close! "Wait, everyone! Look!" He pushed his brother aside and ran to the other edge. A few others began to notice too. "Look! Look, everyone! Look up there! It's him! It's really him! Look! Look!"

Everyone turned their heads and gazed up, astonished!

"Oh, no! No!" the Black Beard Gang thought. "No! No! It couldn't be! It couldn't! It could NOT!" But it was! The mysterious creature! The Phantom Ape! It swung in and landed into the tree. Their worst nightmare! They saw it now, with their own eyes! And now, reader, it was their turn to be afraid.

3

THE BATTLE IN THE LIFE TREE AND THE VERY SEVERE BEATING OF THE APE BULLIES

It was just like out of one of Sebastian's day dreams. The action! The excitement! The surprises! The bad guys, who he'd always wished and hoped someone would stand up to, finally getting a taste of their own medicine!

The creature was about four feet tall, slender, upright and covered in all kinds of curious things that none of the other animals had ever seen before. It wore a black hood and black cape, beneath which shone bright green armor made of alligator skin. Maybe that was one of the bad animals it had killed, like the legends told! The creature also had a turtle shell shield and a bow and arrow. But at the time it was attacking, it was holding a long, pointed staff made of heavy oak. The sight of it was terrifying to the apes! Especially that green armor! For there was nothing that apes were more afraid of than great snakes and lizards. It made all of them begin to panic and scatter.

"Oh no! It's the Phantom Ape! It's real! It's really real! Run away! Run away!"

"I'm not staying to fight that thing! Forget it!"

"Quick, run! Before it eats us! Don't you remember the stories?"

But Old Black Beard wouldn't let them. He was too determined to rule the forest! And he wasn't about to let one little animal spoil his plan—Phantom Ape or not!

"You cowards!" he shouted down at them. "Don't be afrrr-aid! It's just one crrr-eature! Seize him! Seize him, I say! That's an order! Make him suffah!"

"Yes sir!" the bravest ones yelled back.

The mysterious creature, meanwhile, wasn't wasting any time. As soon as it landed in the tree, it leaped down with its staff and delivered such a blow onto one poor ape's head that it went cross eyed and straight to sleep . . . tumbling out of the tree, down into some mud.

"Oh yeah!" cried Sebastian, very impressed. "Pow! Right in the face! Did you see that?" He loved every minute of it.

Three more of the gang fell under our hero's staff after that. Smack! Thwack! Oof! Just like that! And when others tried to jump up onto the branch to tackle it, the mysterious creature batted them away like baseballs, one by one.

It would also use the pointy end of its staff to prick and pry at the apes. And if anyone tried to sneak up on the creature, look out! It would swoosh its staff sideways and downward, tripping their legs out from under them. No one had ever seen anything like this beating before! Fifteen had already fallen out of the tree! And none of them looked like they were planning on getting up again.

"Pow! Oh, yeah!" yelled Sebastian. "Bang! Yeah, get him! Woo! Oh yeah! Pow! Pow! Pow!"

Even Edward was getting into it. All of the good animals were. Everyone except Dorabella, that is. She thought it was too violent for little chicks to see, and was trying to cover Sebastian's eyes.

"Oh, Mrs. Butterfly!" she lamented, hoping to get at least one animal on her side. "Isn't this simply awful?"

But when she turned to her, she saw that the butterfly was cheering too—and possibly even enjoying it more than any of the boy animals were.

"Kill!" she squeaked delightedly. It was half-scary to see and half-cute. "Kill! Kill! Kill! Muah hah hah hah hah! Give it to them! Like that! Hi-ya!"

"Oh goodness . . ." sighed Dorabella.

The hero spotted Lumpy and his friends and used its whip to swing down to save them. Stomper saw it coming and tried to stomp them first, but couldn't. Before his foot came down, the mysterious creature managed to swoop under it and scoop them up. A very close call! It made everyone wonder even more about what kind of creature was under that hood.

"Wow! Look at him go!" Sebastian marvelled. "Did you see that long thing he swung with? What is that? It can't be a tail! It came from his hand! Do you think he's a spider?"

"Don't be ridiculous," replied Edward, sounding like a know-it-all. "He's obviously some sort of flying pig."

Dorabella was more concerned about how they kept referring to it as a boy.

"Hey! Why do you keep saying 'he?' It could be a girl you know . . ."

"Hah! A girl!" Sebastian gawked. "Don't make me laugh! Now, quiet! I'm trying to watch!"

The mysterious creature couldn't be caught no matter how many apes chased after it. Even when Old Black Beard sent his personal bodyguards, it always seemed to slip through their fingers.

"Ooh! Ahh! Ooh Ahh! More apes! More

apes! Ooh Ahh! Ooh Ahh! What are you waiting for? Ooh Ahh! Ooh Ahh! Ooh Ahh! Hey you!" he yelled at one next to him. "What are you doing?" He grabbed him by the ear. "Don't just stand there! Get him! Get him!"

Soon there were apes everywhere, all around the good animals' mysterious hero. The evil king ape was sure that would be enough. But it wasn't! The creature was still too fast for them. Every time they'd try to grab or tackle it, the creature would duck, dodge, roll under or jump over them. Once, the apes even swore they saw it jump on top of an ape's head while in midair, using it like a stepping stone!

"I can't catch him! He's too quick!" yelled one ape.

"Hurry! Someone grab its tail!" yelled another.

"It doesn't have one! It doesn't have one! That's what I keep trying to tell you! Try something else!"

And do you remember, reader, when Edward mentioned how there was a rumor that the creature could weave spider webs? Well, those turned out to be nets it threw at its enemies. The mysterious creature carried them in little mysterious pouches of the very mysterious belt it wore. Sometimes it would throw them at apes who were jumping towards it and catch them that way. Other times, it would throw them down at an open space and use them like a trampoline to jump up to higher places. It seemed uncatchable! Except, that is, for one of the apes . . .

Stomper was able to jump up high without the aid of any rope trampoline. He could do it just by using his big, strong legs.

"One . . . two . . . three!" He counted. And he launched himself up to where the mysterious creature was. When he landed, the whole tree shook and there was nowhere to run or swing to. Stomper had it trapped!

"Ho! Ho! Ho! . . . Hoo! Hoo! Hoo!" he grunted, walking slowly towards his victims. The branch was getting wet with his drool. The mysterious creature nearly slipped on it.

"Ho! Ho! Ho! HO! HO! HO! Come on, Phantom Ape, and fight! Stomper not scared of you! HO! . . . HO! . . . HO! . . ."

It was hard to balance with the branch shaking from the stomps. Lumpy and his friends, who were on our hero's back, were throwing acorns they'd grabbed at Stomper. But they just bounced right off him and made him laugh that stupid laugh even more.

"Blast!" said Sebastian getting worried. "Look at him, he's trapped! We've got to do something! We've got to help! Or he'll be stomped for sure!"

Sebastian didn't care that he was little. While everyone else was busy just watching, he wanted to get involved and do something! So, he looked around and thought of an idea.

"I know!" he said. "I've got it! Watch!"

And he took off running down the branch, fluttering and even flying a little here and there.

"Oh, Sebastian! Do be careful!" yelled his sister, who was ready to follow now if necessary.

"What's gotten into that chick?" said one of the older birds in the tree. "I say! Has he gone mad?"

Sebastian found a large bee hive nested right above where Stomper was standing.

"Hey!" he said to them. "Say, uh . . . Ahem . . . Do you guys mind if I—"

But the bees had already been thinking the same thing.

"Yezzz! DoOoOo it!" they all buzzed together. "We beezzz are ready to defend our tree!"

The queen stepped very carefully and daintily out of the hive and onto the branch where Sebastian was.

"Go on, soldiers! Do your duty! We all remember the war the apes waged on us last time!

Now it's time for—buzzzzz—our revenge! God speed, boyz!"

Then all of the bees yelled "for the queen!" and Sebastian pecked at the top, causing the hive to break off and fall down . . . down . . . right onto Stompers big head! It broke open and they all started stinging him at once. "Hazza! Hazza! Buzz! Buzz! Buzz! Hazza! Take that!" It wasn't long until Stomper lost his balance and fell to the ground. He ran away crying after that, and was never seen again.

"Thanks!" said the mysterious creature, looking up at Sebastian and waving. Sebastian smiled, star-struck, and waved back.

That was the end of the Black Beard Gang. As soon as they saw their strongest ape run off, they fled or limped away along with him.

"Run away! Run away!" was all you could hear besides the now even louder cheering and clapping for the hero—jumping up and down in excitement.

"No! No!" cried Old Black Beard. "Come back, you fools! Don't leave me!"

His plan had failed. His guards were gone and no one was left to defend him. Never before had he ever felt so frustrated or humiliated, reader! He was angry! Furious! But he was no longer scary to anyone.

The mysterious creature spent some time

showboating—flipping through the air, waving, doing tricks and giving high fives. Everyone felt like it was on their side. Everyone trusted it. Even after they saw how dangerous it was.

Out of the corner of its eye, the creature then saw Old Black Beard trying to sneak away. With one crack of its whip and a bounce on one of its trampoline nets, it bounded—flew!— straight up the branch he was on, blocking his path.

"Freeze!" it said.

Then it drew its spear and thrust it towards Black Beard's neck, forcing him to back up until his back was right up against the trunk of the tree.

"Don't move! I'm warning you. Don't try and run!"

4

OLD BLACK BEARD
SURRENDERS

What a strange sounding voice this mysterious creature had! It definitely wasn't an ape. Nor did it sound like a girl animal, as Dorabella had been hoping. The voice was far too deep for that. Everyone wondered and waited in silence.

As you remember, the mysterious hero had defeated the Black Beard Gang. It had their leader, Old Black Beard, pinned up against the trunk of the Life Tree. The creature's spear was pressed firmly against the ape's neck, nearly pricking through the skin.

Old Black Beard had never been so scared in all his life. He was sweating. His knees were shaking. He couldn't even talk properly. And then there was the embarrassment of being defeated. A part of him was actually very glad, reader, that none of his gang was left there to see him this way.

"Boo hoo! Boo hoo! Ho, ho, ho! Ooh ahh! Ooh ahh! P-p-p-please, sir! D-d-d-don't k-k-k-kill me! Ooh ahh!"

"Wow," Sebastian marveled. "Look at him. He's like a big baby."

Many of the animals watching felt almost sorry for Old Black Beard. There were some whispers about how, maybe, he should be let go. But not the hero. He was still very upset.

"Hmm . . . Now, what do you have to say for yourself, thief? Kidnapper!"

He pressed his spear in a little more just to make sure Old Black Beard knew he was serious.

"Ah! Ouch! Ouch! Ouch! Oh, no! Please! I'm . . . ugh . . . I'm sorry! Yes, I surrender! You win! Please! Let me go . . ."

"Hmm . . . just like you were going to let Lumpy and his friends go? And return their bananas you stole?"

"Ugh . . . Ugh . . ." stuttered the villain, sweating more. He didn't have a clue what to say.

"Yeah, right," answered the mysterious creature. "I didn't think so! Nope, you're under arrest!"

"Arrest? Oh! No! No! How horrible! How

lamentable! Alas! Alas! Anything but that! Ugh . . ." Then he whispered. "Ugh . . . ahem . . . what does 'arrest' mean?"

"It means I'm going to take you away! You took Lumpy and his friends as prisoners. So, now you're going to be their prisoners. I plan on taking you over there myself."

"Oh no, no! Please! No! Anything but that! They hate me! Who knows what they'll do to me!? I'm a goner if you take me back! Oh, boo hoo! Please don't, sir!"

"Well, you should have thought of that before you kidnapped their favorite prince."

"Prince?" Sebastian thought. "Lumpy was a prince? I didn't know that."

Lumpy jumped off the mysterious hero's back and onto his head. He posed nobly, like a handsome statue.

"You see?" said the mysterious creature.

"What? You've got to be kidding me! A little runt like him? A prince!? No way! I'm the prince! Me! Me! I'm the king!"

"Not anymore you're not," replied the hero defiantly. "You're through. Your reign of terror is over."

Hearing this really upset Old Black Beard. To be spoken to in such a way was something he just wasn't used to. And, for a moment, he forgot that he'd just been overpowered.

"What! What did you say! Me? Through? Guards! Seize him! I shall have you whipped for your insolence! Guards! Gua- Ah! Ghup!"

But he suddenly remembered that there was a spear to his throat, and that his guards had all run away. So, he quickly covered his mouth before he could say anymore.

"Ugh, I mean . . . I'm sorry for kidnapping your charming little friends. Heh, heh . . . Ahem!"

"Hmph. Well, sorry, but it's too late for that. You can apologize to them as their prisoner. And maybe if you're nice, then—just maybe— they'll forgive you and let you go. Now, let's see . . . hmm . . . where are my handcuffs . . ."

The mysterious creature took out a special extra strong rope he'd made. But in order to put them on Old Black Beard, he had to put away his spear. He reattached it to the harness on his back.

"Alright, come here."

Old Black Beard knew this would be his only chance. The mysterious creature was unarmed. He gave the hero one of his hands to make it seem like he was giving up. But as the hero slipped it on, he very sneakily raised his other hand up, ready to chop the hero with it. He thought he had him for sure. With all of his rage, he then thrust it down as hard as he could, aiming for the mysterious creature's head.

"Die, Phantom Ape! Die!" he yelled. "You'll never take me alive! Do you hear me!? Now, witness my power! Hiii-yaaaa! Agh! Oof!"

But in the blink of an eye, Old Black Beard went from almost hitting our hero, to being on his back. It happened that fast! The mysterious creature caught the chop and punched him square in the stomach.

"Wow! Look at that speed!" exclaimed Sebastian. "He's so fast! I didn't even see him move! Did you?"

All you could hear after that was the sound of Old Black Beard moaning and groaning.

"Ohh . . . Ooh!"

"Hmph, nice try," said the hero, crossing his arms. "But you're going to have to do better than that if you want to beat me."

Old Black Beard lay on his back, dumbfounded and stunned that such a blow could be delivered by a creature so small. He didn't even feel scared anymore, but curious like everyone else—curious about what this creature was, and what it looked like under its hood.

"Who . . ." he said, while gasping for air and coughing, "who . . . who . . . are . . . you? What are you!?" He felt at this point like he had to know.

The hero sensed this. He looked around and sensed that it was what everyone else was thinking too, hearing all their whispers. So, he decided to remove his hood. What the animals saw shocked them.

It wasn't a bird. It wasn't an ape. It wasn't a spider. No, it wasn't a flying pig either, like Edward had guessed. It was something else altogether that no animal in that wild forest had ever seen before. It was a human. A boy. He had long, shaggy, dusty brown hair and dark blue eyes. His skin was white, but very tanned and darkened from the hot forest sun.

"Oh, goodness!" said Dorabella and some of the other girl birds. "He's so handsome!"

"Yes, I wonder if he has a girlfriend!" said another.

"I saw him first!" said yet another.

The boy animals all thought he looked tough and brave, like they wanted to be. Everyone was astonished. Even Old Black Beard, though he would never admit it. And everyone started cheering again.

"Well, then," said the boy, walking over to the old villain, who was too ashamed by that point to even look him in the eye. He bent down and put the handcuffs on him. "Time to go."

Then he whistled and everyone saw a wolf

down below pull up to the base of the tree with a sled. The boy took his whip out and looked for the bananas, which were a few branches over, all wrapped up in a giant leaf.

"Hii-yaa!"

With just one crack of it, he split the leaf open. Bananas burst out and poured down everywhere, like candy falling from a piñata. Anyone who wanted could reach out and grab one. Lumpy stuffed about three in his mouth at the same time. But most of the fruit fell into the sled, where he was trying to aim them.

"Wait, wait! I can explain!" whimpered Old Black Beard, making all manner of ridiculous excuses for his crimes as the hero dragged him along the branch. "There's been a mistake! I didn't rob them. They robbed me! Ouch!" His behind was dragging along the branch, getting pricked each step of the way by thorns that were growing, feeling like the very Life Tree itself was getting some revenge on him too. "Ouch! Ouch! Ouch! You don't understand! Ouch! They made me do it! Youch! I wouldn't have had to take it from them if they had just given the bananas to me when I asked! Ouch! I wanted it, you see! And they wouldn't give it to me! Me! ME!"

"Yeah? And what's so special about you?"

Old Black Beard was shocked and appalled

by the question.

"Hah!" he scoffed. "Isn't it obvious? Look at me. Look at me!"

The boy stopped pulling Old Black Beard for a moment and looked down at him.

"Who wouldn't want to give me their things? Look at me! You'd have to be crazy! Don't you see?"

But, despite looking really hard, the boy didn't.

"No," he answered awkwardly, raising an eyebrow. And he started pulling him again.

"Oh!" the old ape scoffed some more. "Oh! The nerve! Insolence! How dare you! Ouch! Ouch! How dare you!"

Some of the animals began throwing bananas at his head, too.

"Ouch! Stop it! Stop it immediately! You are ruffians! All of you!"

Finally, they got to the end of the branch. The hero kicked Old Black Beard in the behind, which by then had so many thorns in it that it looked like a porcupine. He fell down with all the bananas into the back of the sled. Then, with the three apes still on his back, the hero jumped down too, giving more high fives to his new fans on the way down—all of whom were trying to push each other out of the way to get close.

"Hey! Move!"

"I want to see him, too!"

"Over here! Don't forget about me!"

The hero jumped up front with the wolf and pulled the sled away, making sure to wave to as many of the animals in the Life Tree as possible —the clapping and cheering getting louder and louder, until he finally disappeared. What a day it had been for the creatures in that tree, reader! What a day, indeed!

Young Sebastian flapped and chirped until he got so tired, he could flap and chirp no more.

"Well!" he sighed, out of breath. "That was something, wasn't it!?"

He looked over at Edward who was now feeling quite embarrassed for teasing Sebastian earlier. Sebastian couldn't help rubbing it in.

"So!" he said, crossing his arms triumphantly, "Now do you believe me, Edward?"

Edward didn't like being wrong. He glared stubbornly at Sebastian. Sebastian glared right back. But then they both realized they were far too happy to fight, and their frowns turned into smiles! Instead of arguing, they grabbed their sister and all three of them started hopping up and down together, for the very first time in their lives feeling hopeful about what the future might bring!

5

THE JOURNEY HOME

That's what happened at the Life Tree that day, reader! And it had the whole forest in an uproar as news spread about the new creature everyone was talking about. The three little apes were saved! Old Black Beard was arrested and his gang was no more! The forest in the great valley was finally at peace.

But little did everyone know, this was only just the beginning. There was another villain, even more powerful than Old Black Beard, who lived far over the mountains. He planned on invading and destroying the forest—and eventually taking over the whole world: a villain known as the Dragon King.

This story is about that Dragon King, reader, and the adventure that two young heroes —a boy and a girl—went on to stop him.

It would be the first of many adventures they would go on to save the world. Each more exciting and magical than the last! The book you are now holding is but one of many in a vast library that chronicles them.

But of all the adventures in the collection, reader, this first one about the Dragon King is by far the most important—because this is the one that shows how it all got started. Who were our hero and heroine? Where did they come from? How did they meet and become friends? As you'll soon see, the adventures came very close to never happening at all.

In fact, if even one little thing you are about to read hadn't occurred, not only would our two heroes never have met, but the young forest boy here wouldn't even have left the great valley! In the beginning of our story, he was perfectly happy in the wild. He didn't even know there was an "outside the valley."

But something happened that day after the battle at the Life Tree, reader. Something that changed our hero forever and set him upon a new path of exploration over the horizon.

I will begin, first, by telling you this story. Then, in the next volume, I will tell you the tale of our heroine and how she got involved in all these adventures too.

It all started at precisely the moment our hero was coming around a bend after the battle. As you remember, he had just finished saving Lumpy and his friends, seizing back the stolen fruit and capturing grumpy Old Black Beard, former boss of the Black Beard Gang. He was pulling them all through the grass on a sled, accompanied by a great grey wolf. Lumpy was fast asleep with his belly full. Old Black Beard had an apple tied into his mouth to keep him from talking.

They came to a meadow with a stream of crystal-clear water running through it. Suddenly, the glimmer of the sun's reflection off it caught the boy's eye, and he couldn't help but decide it was a good place to rest. They pulled in and let go of the reigns, exhausted. Then they ran over to have a drink.

It was very funny to see. He dropped down on all fours and started licking it up, in exactly the same manner the wolf was. He even dunked his head in and started shaking himself dry like a wolf. If he'd been covered in fur, you might not even think he was a boy at all.

The reason for all of this very odd behavior was, of course, because our hero was raised by a wolf—the same one he was with now. She found him as an abandoned baby nine years ago and brought him up just like a cub. They were very different, but had been best friends ever since.

After they drank their fill and cooled off, they fell backward onto the grass to relax in the light. It was our hero's favorite thing to do. He cupped his hand over his eyes and looked up at the sun, thinking all sorts of funny thoughts.

I wonder what it's made of? How did it get there? Where does it go?

Our hero loved wondering. If he had the time, he might have done so all day. His wolf friend, however, felt very differently.

"Hey!" she said to him suddenly, whacking him over the head with her paw. "Stop it!"

It was what she always did when she saw the boy thinking, and this might have been the biggest difference between them.

"Ouch! Hey! What was that for? Stop what?"

"That! Thinking! You know I don't like it when you do that."

The wolf's name was Ava. And ever since he was toddler, she discouraged thinking as much as she could.

"Always remember, if you think, you hesitate. And if you hesitate, you're dead. It's why that one big ape almost beat you. You hesitated. You should have charged in. That's the last thing he'd expect."

"Oh . . . sorry," replied the boy.

Ava had taught him everything she knew about fighting. She brought him up as a warrior. Thinking, she believed, was for dummies. For if you had to think, it meant you didn't know. She felt the same way about any kind of fun or playing. All a big waste of time. She wasn't a very nice wolf at all.

"And all that showboating! You know I don't like that either. You lost focus! There could have still been someone around to attack you. Get in and get out. No funny business. Hey! Are you listening to me?"

The sun had caught the boy's attention again. He was very forgetful of her rules.

"Hmm . . ." he sighed as he started wondering again. "Hmm . . ."

"Oh, great. Here we go again . . ."

"I wonder where it goes . . . What do you think, Ava?"

He looked over at her, but she wasn't interested. The only things she ever liked to talk about was war.

"Where does the sun go? What a foolish question!"

"Aw, come on. I don't think it is. I'm curious!"

"Curiosity killed the cat. I know—because I'm the one who eats cats! Or at least I used to, back in the old days when you were more fun."

"I bet it's somewhere warm," the boy continued, growing even more curious. "Being warm itself, that's probably where it would want to be. Maybe there is a place where it's always warm, somewhere where food and flowers grow all year long, where there's no snow—except maybe on mountains—and no winter. Ah," he sighed. "No winter. Wouldn't that be nice?"

The boy rolled over and looked at his friend, hoping to get her opinion. But instead, she just rolled her eyes.

"Hmph. Whatever. Fool . . ."

She then sat up and headed back to the sled. "No, it's silly—the whole thing! Now, come on. Let's get going."

"Wait, do we have to? Just a little longer . . ."

He was so comfortable lying there under the sun. But he knew Ava didn't care. He could almost feel her eyes on him, glaring.

"Alright," he said. "I'm coming . . . I'm coming . . ."

Our two heroes hopped back up to the front of the sled and pulled it the rest of the way to Lumpy's ape village. They crossed over great and vast fields of flowers, around long winding cliffs on the sides of mountains, and took secret passages and short cuts that led through underground ice caves or behind waterfalls—the same waterfalls with rainbows over them that young Sebastian would see in the distance and dream about. Before long, they found themselves in a lush wood with soft grass and black soil. It was no wonder the good apes chose to build their home here. There were many berries and fruit you could pick right off the ground all summer long. As they approached, they were greeted with even more cheering than when they left the Life Tree that morning.

"Look, he's back!"

"There's Lumpy! He saved them!"

"I knew he would!"

"And there's Old Black Beard, all tied up! He got him!"

"And our bananas! Hurray!"

All of the little girl apes then rushed up into the trees to shower them with white flower petals, making it look like it was snowing. The young males all ran to try and get a glimpse of the hero up close.

"Get out of my way!"

"Ouch! Quit pushing me! I was here first!"

When the sled finally stopped, it was immediately surrounded by a crowd full of curiosity, questions and excitement.

"Oh, hey everyone!" said the boy pulling up. He was so used to this sort of welcome now that he hardly noticed anymore. "Umm, how are you all doing?"

"Hey! Is that your stinger?" asked one of the little apes.

"No, it's just a stick, see? I call it a spear."

"Can I see it?"

"Sure, but you have to be careful. It's sharp."

"Can you really fly?"

"Nope. It just looks like it sometimes. I've got this whip, you see? I can swing with it. And I can make trampolines. Sometimes I can glide, too. But my last glider broke. I've got to make a new one."

"Ooh!" they all sighed delightedly.

"Hey! Where's your tail?"

"Don't have one."

"Where did it go?"

"I don't know—must have fallen off or something."

"Can you really go invisible?"

"Nope—just good at hiding."

The boy enjoyed talking to other animals and answering questions, even if he didn't always have the answer. But Ava hated it.

"Hey everyone! Look! It's Ava! She's a hero too!"

"What? No, I'm not. Leave me alone. Hey, get off me!"

Many of the apes surrounded her and

started trying to put flowers into her fur, or kissing her on her cheek. She hated every minute of it.

"Ugh—yuck! Gross!"

But it was a part of the job, and she knew it.

"Pugh! Apes . . ." she muttered.

The crowd's attention then drew to a voice coming from behind it—a deep and somewhat funny sounding voice coming from one of the adults. You could hear them pushing their way towards the sled.

"Out'f my way! Out'f my way! Ooh ooh!"

The boy recognized it. It was Lumpy's father.

"Ooh ooh! Grr! Where is he!? Where is he!?" he growled. He seemed grouchy. "Where is Lumpy!?"

He pushed and shoved his way through the crowd. Sometimes he took a little apeling and threw him over his shoulder to get through to the sled. Though, that was quite a normal thing for apes to do, even when they weren't upset. Any apeling he'd toss would end up landing safely on a branch above.

"Where is he? Where is he? Do you know where he is?" he'd ask before tossing someone. "No? Hi-ya! What about you? Or you! Hiya! Hiya! Where is he! Where is that little fur ball!" He pushed through, all the way to where Lumpy was sleeping. "Ooh! Ooh! Ooh! When I find him, I'm going to wring his little . . ."

That's when Lumpy awoke. He yawned and stretched his tiny little arms—then sat up. His father was about to scold him. But he found that he couldn't. Right before he tried, his heart melted and his eyes began to shed tears of joy. Instead, he reached out to hug him.

"Aww, come 'ere son," he sighed. "Come'ere! Give your father a hug! Oh! Boo hoo! We missed you! I'm sorry for yellin'."

And Lumpy jumped into his arms. So did the other two little apes when their families came.

"You're safe! Look at you!" said all the mothers and fathers. "You're alright! Thank you!" they cried turning to our hero. "Thank you so much!"

It put the biggest smile on our hero's face and the deepest joy in his heart to see them all together where they belonged.

"You're welcome! Anytime!"

But soon the crowd started to grow so big that the boy, Ava and the sled looked like they were getting swallowed up by them. It was getting out of control. So, Lumpy's father had to break it up.

"Alright, that's enough! The show's over!

Break it up! Leave'm alone! He needs to relax! Go on! Scram!"

The apelings listened and started running off together to play. Ava shook out all the flowers they put in her hair and stuck around the sled to keep an eye on Old Black Beard, who was still tied up.

"Come on, my young friend!" said the father putting his arm around the boy. "We'd better get you indoors before anyone else sees ya'. Especially the young ladies round 'ere. You remember last time! Hmm, I know—you can come to my house! Yes! Come this way! There is something I want to show you!"

6

LUMPY'S FAMILY

L umpy's father led the boy to their little home under a tree. It was very warm and cozy. There were soft places to sit and beds anyone could hop up and nap on. Roots from the tree came down through the roof for the little children apes to play or hang on.

Lumpy had many brothers and sisters who ran up to the boy and greeted him with hugs and big monkey kisses on his cheek. They took him by the hand and led him over to their mother, who was resting on a little bed. She was cradling something that everyone seemed excited about.

"What was it?" our hero wondered.

Lumpy's father then went over and scooped it up, letting out a great sigh of joy, and brought it over.

"Ah, look! Look! Here he is! My new son! Here! Hold'm! Take a look for yourself!"

The boy very reluctantly put his arms out. He had never actually held a baby before. He would have asked about the right way of doing it, but it was already too late. Before he was ready, the father extended his arms and dropped the child. The boy caught him just in time. The baby had big round brown eyes and short fuzzy hair. He had the cutest, tiniest little ears, a little nose and an adorable expression of curiosity as he tried to work out why his mother's face had suddenly changed.

"Goo gah! Goo gah!" it babbled.

"Ah, you hear that!" said the father. "He almost has his 'ooh ahh' down. Must o' been practice'n! Good job, kiddo!"

Our hero's eyes lit up and he smiled delightedly. What a charming little creature! He had always loved looking at babies, but very rarely ever got the opportunity. Animals in the wild tended to be very careful about that. They wouldn't let you anywhere near them unless they trusted you.

"Oh, wow!" said our hero. "Look! He's so small . . ."

"Hmm? Small? Oh, yes! Very small. But quick and sneaky! Even at that age, if you don't keep an eye on 'em!" answered the father. "Especially Lumpy! He was always run'n and leap'n and crawl'n off! He ran out of our whole village once! Had to wrestle a great snake to save him."

"Really?" asked the boy. "You fought a snake?"

"Oh, yes! I had to. And gave him a good walloping, too! He never knew what hit him!"

"Oh please," interrupted Lumpy's mother then, with a sigh, "that snake had you so tied up, you couldn't move. It was me who pulled you out, remember?"

"Alright!" muttered the father. "Anyways, it's not important how I did it—ahem, I mean how *we* did it. The point is that *he* got away and *we* got him home safe again!"

"But you could have died," said the boy concerned. "Snakes that size eat apes."

It was one thing for our hero to fight a beast like that. He had weapons and training—not to mention, a fully grown wolf at his side. But one of the Brumbledumb apes? It was true that they were strong, but they weren't warriors.

"Yes, yes! I suppose I could have," answered the father. "But there are more important things than not dying."

Lumpy's mother nodded in agreement.

"Yeah, I guess so," said our hero.

"Oh, that reminds me! It's why I brought you here. You know how you're always helping us? Well, I've decided to name this one after you, in your honor! Er, the two of us, I mean." He glanced at his wife. "The one you're hold'n! What do ya' say?"

The boy stood frozen and surprised. No one had ever asked him such a question before. He thought about it and then looked down to see if maybe the little one had an opinion.

"What do you think, baby?"

The apeling didn't seem very enthusiastic. Neither did he seem very happy being held by him. What happened to his mother? Who was this imposter? The baby started to squirm and tear up. Our hero saw this and quickly returned him.

"Oh! Sorry! Here you go . . ."

"The Invisible Hand!" yelled out the father, "That will be his name! Handy, for short!"

"Andy," said the mother correcting him.

"Ugh . . . ahem . . . alright . . . Andy then!"

No one actually knew what our hero's real name was yet, reader. Like the "Phantom Ape," the "Invisible Hand" was merely a nickname. Not even our hero knew his real name. He hadn't come with one when Ava had found him as a baby. Nor had he answered to any name, except with crying. So, for a long time Ava just called him "cry baby," and other things she'd make up as she raised him. Then, as he grew and finally emerged, crawling from their cave, other animals saw and joined in. He didn't always like or understand the names he was called. The "Invisible Hand" was particularly peculiar. But he did always find them interesting.

"Yes, yes! Andy!" the father continued, feeling very proud of his decision.

"Sure!" said the boy.

"Who knows, maybe when he grows up, he will have your strength!"

"Yeah, maybe!"

"Which reminds me . . ." The father seemed to need a lot of reminding. "Why don't you have any little ones yet?"

"Hmm? What do you mean?" the boy answered.

"You know—babies! Kids! Why, when I was your age, I already had three!"

"Oh . . . I don't know . . ."

The father then shuffled over and began whispering to him up close. Maybe even a little too close.

"Um . . . It's not because of your, uh . . . little *problem*, is it?"

He glanced down at the boy's body and looked concerned. The boy looked too. But he didn't see anything.

"What problem?" he asked curiously.

"Well . . . you know . . ." said the father,

trying to be as polite as possible—and not at all awkward. "Well . . . I mean . . . well, look at you! Look! Your body! You're all skin! No hair anywhere! Except on your head!" As the father spoke, he pinched the boy on his arm, which made him jump a bit. "It gets so cold at night. I don't know how you sleep, being like that!"

"Oh, I see . . ."

It was something the boy sometimes wondered about as well.

"Anyways," the father continued, clearing his throat. "Ahem . . . I want you to know that it's *not* a problem anymore. My sister has had'r eye on you for quite some time! And I've spoken to'r! And she's said she'd be will'n to be patient of it! Come!" said the father, taking the boy by the arm. "Come! Come and see for yourself . . ."

He led him to a window. Our hero was feeling even more confused.

"Huh? What? Who? Where?"

"Shh! Look! Over there!"

He pointed outside. The boy squinted and cupped his hand over his eyes to see better.

"Look! He! He! Do you see now?"

There was a girl ape out there. An enormous one! Tall and round! And she was looking right back at him!

"He! He! Well, what do you think?"

Our hero didn't understand what he was

asking until he saw the ape girl start batting her eyelashes, giggling and waving at him—making kissy faces!

"Agh!" the boy yelled, horrified.

"Well?" said the father rubbing his hands together, getting very excited. "Well, come on! Tell me! What do you think? Pretty, ain't she? Just look at that beard! And those whiskers! And that hairy chest! Enough to keep you both warm, if you follow my mean'n . . . He! He! He!"

"Agh!" shrieked the boy again. He tumbled back this time and tripped over a root. He fell all the way back onto his head.

"Uhhh . . . uhhh . . . ummm . . ." he squeaked as he tried to scramble back to his feet. "Uhhh . . . ummm . . . no . . . no . . . no, thank you . . ."

Lumpy's father felt very puzzled and surprised.

"What! Really? Are you sure?"

"Yes! Yes!"

"She'll be disappointed, you know . . ."

The boy had to catch his breath.

"That's . . . that's okay . . ."

"Well, alright then—if you say so."

The father went back to the window and gave the girl ape a thumbs down. She was very disappointed indeed and ran off somewhere to cry.

"You will at least stay for dinner, though, won't you?"

Now that was something the boy *was* interested in. He clamped his palms together and licked his lips. He was just about to say "yes" when suddenly an ominous voice from behind them spoke:

"Not tonight."

The boy, the father and the whole ape family spun around, where in the corner they saw Ava. None of them knew how long she'd been sitting there listening.

"Woah!" said the ape father. "Ava, what are you trying to do? Give me a heart attack? Sneaky monkey! Well, you're welcome to stay too of course!"

"No, thanks," she replied coldly. "Come on, kid. We're leaving. Now."

She looked up and directed everyone's attention to a window in the ceiling where dark clouds could be seen forming. It was the last day of fall and she didn't like getting back to the cave before it was too late.

"Ho! Ho! Wow! Would you look at that! Ava is right! Yes, it looks like a winter storm will be roll'n in soon. You two best be getting home quick! Unless you want to move in with us for the winter. We got room!"

Ava turned around without even caring to

answer and started walking out. But the boy didn't want to go yet. He had worked so hard that day and wanted to rest and be with his friends, not go back to the cave. He hated winter—more than anything. The winters were particularly harsh in this forest, reader. Everything would freeze. It was almost impossible to find any food. All he could do was gather as much of it together as possible and do his best to keep it fresh before it spoiled—or try to eat as much as he could beforehand. That's why he had a much bigger belly right now than usual. A cold shiver went down his spine as he thought about going back.

"We can stay just a little longer, can't we?" he asked quietly with his stomach rumbling.

Ava stalled in the doorway. "No," she answered. Then she was gone.

7

HENRY THE BEAR

All of the Brumbledumbs gathered at the border to say goodbye. They offered our hero some of their bananas as a gift, but he didn't take any. Winter had nearly arrived and the boy knew the large family would need every one of them to survive. Especially the little ones.

"Thank you, everyone!" he shouted. "See you in spring! Goodbye! I'll miss you!"

"Thank you!" the apes all shouted back. "You're welcome any time! Goodbye! Stay warm!"

It was a lovely end to another lovely visit. And when our heroes left, there were many more animals who came to say goodbye. For now that the Black Beard Gang had been defeated—as well as almost all of the others bullies—the forest now felt safe again. The good animals could come out and play one last time before the seasons changed.

"Hello!" they would squeak as the boy passed by. "Thank you for saving us!"

"You're welcome!" he would reply.

Some animals would even come right up and let the boy pet them. Or, if they were small enough, they would sit on his shoulder as he walked, regaling him with news and gossip about the forest. Who was being naughty? Who was being nice? What kinds of new villains might be emerging? Which way home should our hero go? And so on.

"Hey! Psst! Listen! There are some apples over there! No one's seen them yet!" a little bird whispered in his ear.

"Thanks!"

Or . . .

"Be careful, sonny, there is quicksand ahead . . ."

It was the old turtles who gave him that advice.

"Sure," he replied. "Thank you for telling—"

"Young whipper snappers! Run'n round without any patience! Darn kids ain't got no virtue, I tells ye! No virtue! What's wrong with parents these days?"

"Oh, umm . . . that's too bad. I'm sorry to hear that."

"Never mind that, sonny. You best be heading home."

"Right!"

"Wisely and slow, now. They stumble who run."

"I will. Bye, Mr. Turtle!"

But along the way there was one animal who caught the boy's attention more than any other: his old friend, Henry the Bear. He was large, had thick bushy brown fur and was always smiling and singing merrily wherever he went. Our hero heard him and rushed over to say hello.

La! La! La! Berries! Berries!
Squash em in my mouth!
Row after row!
On our way down south!
Yummy, yummy berries!
Apples, bananas, peas and cherries!
What better place than in . . .
Bears' bellies!
La! La! La!

Ava wanted to ignore it and just keep going. But it was too late.

"Henry! Hey, over here!" the boy called out.

"Oh! Hello, there!" Henry answered. "Why, what a wonderful surprise! Ho! Ho! Ho!"

Henry the Bear was one of our hero's favorite animals in the whole forest. He met him when he was very young. Henry taught him how to fish and do many other tricks. "If you let the little fishies go, they'll grow into bigger fishies later for you to eat," the boy remembered him saying. Henry had kept the boy close ever since.

Ava, on the other hand, didn't like Henry at all. She thought his singing was annoying and that his laugh was stupid. And he laughed a lot because he was always tickling himself.

"Ah, hah! Ah, hah, hah, hah, hah! Muah! Hah! Hah! Hah!"

Just like that.

Ava put up with him when he was around, but was always eager to get away as soon as possible.

"Yeah! It's a nice surprise to see you too!" answered the boy. "How's your summer been?"

"Oh, simply un-bear-able!" answered Henry with a chuckle. "The ground is dry. There isn't a single blueberry anywhere! Not even in the meadows. I haven't eaten a thing in three days."

"Oh, I see," said the boy, feeling concerned.

"But you seem to be doing quite well for yourself. Yes! You are much taller than I saw you last! A plump belly! And—such nice round thighs . . . He! He!"

The boy glanced down at himself.

"Thanks . . . I guess . . ." he answered, shrugging.

"You are very welcome! So polite, too."

Henry patted the boy on his head with his great big bear paw.

"Maybe I can help you?" our hero asked.

He went into one of his pockets and pulled out a little pouch.

"I've been collecting acorns. See?"

Henry's eyes lit up.

"Oh! Acorns! Wow! I can see that you have! Very clever! Yes! Look at that, Ava! Now, that is SMART isn't it?"

Ava rolled her eyes.

"Here," said the boy, putting his hand out. "Have some."

"No! Oh, no! I couldn't! You've earned those fair and square. You keep them. Besides—Heh! Heh! We bears prefer softer . . . juicier things . . . like fish or honey. Acorns would only give me a belly ache. And you wouldn't want that, now, would you?"

"No . . ." said the boy sadly. He slouched and looked ashamed that he didn't have anything else to give.

"Aw! Don't worry about me, bucko. Your old

Uncle Henry will be alright. I always am! Muah! Hah! Hah!"

Henry patted him on the head again and playfully messed up his hair. He burst out laughing and started tickling himself. Then he started tickling the boy and made him laugh too, to cheer him up.

"Ho! Ho! Ho! Ho! Tickle! Tickle! He! He! I wouldn't mind your company, though! Which way are you headed, my boy? Maybe your old Uncle Henry could come, too! He! He!"

"Which way do you think we're headed?" asked Ava grouchily. She couldn't take the laughing and playing anymore. "Overgrown weasel! It's nearly winter. We're going home! Where else!?"

"Oh, really? What a coincidence! I'm going that way, too! And, yes, it is almost winter, isn't it? Silly me! Look at the time! I must have forgotten!" Henry was still having fun tickling the boy, who was rolling in laughter from it. Our hero liked that game. "Look! Everyone is out looking for food to survive, but me! What a fool I am! He! He! He!"

"No. You can't come with us. Buzz off! Go and annoy someone else."

"Aw, come on Ava," said the boy, getting back up. "It'll be fun. I want him to come. I haven't seen Henry in a long time. Besides, he's my friend."

Henry smiled a great big bear smile at Ava, showing all of his teeth. There was something strange about this bear. She didn't trust him.

"Yes, come on, Ava! Don't be such a spoil sport. We'll get the boy home safe. We just want to have a little fun on the way, that's all. Sing a little! Talk! I've got some new jokes I could tell you guys! Ho! Ho! Ho!"

Ava looked at the boy, who seemed very eager for Henry to come. She didn't like the idea one bit. That's when Henry whispered something to her.

"Psst . . . Hey, come on. Give the kid a break. You know he has a hard winter ahead of him this year. We both know it could be his last. Don't spoil this for him. He's a good boy and deserves a laugh or two. You've trained him well. Just give him a break just this once. Whaddya say, old pal?"

He reached out to pat Ava on her head too, but stopped when he saw the look in her eye, as if she'd bite him. No one pet Ava—ever.

Nevertheless, Henry did have a point. He got her thinking. Maybe it wasn't such a bad idea after all. The boy had worked hard and done well. Besides, with Henry around, they might even be able to get there faster and safer.

It was the only redeeming thing about him, in her opinion. No one ever tried to ambush them when Henry was nearby.

"Alright, fine," she finally relented.

"Really? Oh, yeah! Great!" the boy exclaimed. "Did you hear that, Henry? You can come!"

He hugged his bear friend tightly.

"Hurray!" Henry cheered with a chuckle. "Ho! Ho! Ho! You're right, my boy! She said so, indeed! Ho! Ho! Ho! What a great friend! Come on! Let's go!"

"Yeah!"

They turned around and started walking together. Finally, they could get moving. That's all Ava really wanted at that point. But no sooner had they taken their first steps, then Henry suddenly stopped again.

"Oh! Wait!"

Our two heroes halted with him.

"What is it, Henry?" the boy asked.

"Make it quick," said Ava.

Henry cleared his throat. He seemed a little different than usual. But Ava couldn't figure out what it was.

"Ahem! Well, nothing really. I just thought of an idea. That's all."

"What?" asked the boy.

"Err—well, what about if we go . . . this way . . . instead . . . over here. Heh! Heh!"

"That way? Hmm . . ." It was something of an odd request. Even the boy thought so. "Why?" he asked.

"Yeah, why?" Ava asked too, but with more suspicion.

"Oh, you know . . . it's just a little easier . . . for these old legs o' mine. Not quite as rocky. It's shorter too."

"And more dangerous," added Ava.

"Not with me around it ain't. Heh! Heh! I don't mean to intrude, of course. It's up to you. We can go any way you please. I just thought you wanted to get home sooner than later. Perhaps I was wrong."

"Sure, we can go that way, Henry," answered the boy. He felt bad that he couldn't give Henry any food earlier. But at least he could help make the trip easier for him. "Especially if you're around. What could go wrong?"

Henry felt very touched and giggled.

"Aw, you are very kind." Then he hugged the boy again. "What a good, good boy you are!"

Ava didn't like the idea. But the storm was blowing in fast. She didn't want to waste any more time. The sooner they got home, the better.

"Alright then! It's settled!" Henry shouted out excitedly before she could answer. He wagged his stubby little tale. "Hah! Follow me! Your Uncle Henry will lead the way. Mauh, hah, hah! Come on, Ava! Pick up your feet! Quit doddling back there! Muah! Hah! Hah! Muah hah, hah, hah, hah!"

8

THE TUNNEL TO SNAKE VALLEY

The only thing the boy ever found odd about Henry the Bear was how he very often broke into fits of uncontrollable laughter—even when nothing funny had happened.

"Brah! Hah! Hah! Hah! . . . Brah! Hah! Hah! Hah! Hah! Hah! . . . Ooh! Hoo! Hoo! Hah! Hah! . . . Hah! Hah! Hah! . . ."

Though usually, it was because of the stories or jokes he'd tell.

"And then!" he would say as they walked, "I fell so in love with her . . . Brah! Hah! Hah! Hah! . . . that I began chasing her around . . . Brah! Hah! Hah! Poor thing! I think she thought I was trying to eat her! Brah! Hah! Hah! Brah! Hah! Hah! . . ."

The boy didn't understand most of Henry's jokes. They were too strange. But when he saw

Henry laugh at them, he laughed too. For of all his favorite things, there was nothing that pleased him more than seeing his friends happy.

Ava, on the other hand, didn't care for his songs or jokes at all. She thought they were silly. So, as they walked, she would trail silently behind as the lookout.

"Could you two buffoons please keep your cackling to a minimum? You're going to wake up the tigers!"

"Ah, relax Ava," said Henry as though she were spoiling all the fun. "You're almost home. We just need to pass through this little tunnel here first. But beware! He! He! The way is treacherous. Many pits! The slightest misstep may lead you hurtling to your doom. Brah! Hah! Hah! Hah!"

The boy didn't see what was so funny about that, but he did as he was told. They went into the tunnel and stepped very carefully. It was dark and full of large cracks you could fall through. Sometimes thunder from the approaching storm would make everything shake. It made a deep rumble and echo that Henry said sounded like his hungry belly. He tickled himself all the way down and hummed. Many times, Ava thought about throwing him down one of the pits. Our hero just focused on not slipping.

At one point, he did almost slip and fall. They turned a corner to where some bats were hanging upside down. They awoke and startled them. Bats started flying everywhere. Shooing them away made him stumble over a rock. Our hero nearly went down a crack, but was caught by Henry just in time.

"Careful, laddy!" he said. His voice echoed loudly "Brah! Hah! Hah! Oh my! That was a close one. Brah! Hah! Hah!"

The boy gulped.

"Thanks!"

Henry lifted and dropped him safely back on the path.

"Fool!" chided Ava. "Watch your step!"

"Sorry."

"Whose idea was it to come in here anyway?" Ava asked. "I don't remember this tunnel."

"Oh, 'tis a secret tunnel. Tee! He! He! Only us bears know about."

"Well, I don't like it one bit," Ava answered.

"Hah! Where's your sense of adventure? We're having fun! Aren't we, my boy?"

Henry smiled with all of his teeth again.

"Yeah, I guess . . ." our hero answered.

"Come on," said Ava. "How much longer to Snake Valley? Our cave isn't far from there. You said this way would be faster."

"Oh, yes. Anytime now. The tunnel leads right to it. There is even a song about it. Shall I sing it for you?"

"No!" snapped Ava.

The boy wasn't sure he wanted Henry to either. There wasn't much light. He couldn't see well. He had to focus on the ground or he would slip again for sure.

"Suit yourselves!" laughed Henry. "It matters not. Besides, we're already here! And, by golly, right in time for the sunset!" Henry darted out excitedly. "Come on. I'll race you!" They both ran now that they could see. The tunnel led out to a cliff that overlooked the whole rocky valley. "Oh, wow! Oh, my! Beautiful! Beautiful! Isn't it?"

The boy liked sunsets too. Both of them stood astonished.

"Well? What do you think?" asked Henry.

"It's a great spot! And thanks for the shortcut," our hero answered.

"It's my pleasure," Henry said tenderly. He saw that Ava wasn't out of the tunnel yet. He took the opportunity to speak alone with the boy.

"You know . . ." he said, suddenly becoming serious. The boy looked up at him and listened closely. "I . . . I don't have many friends . . ."

"Hmm? What do you mean, Henry?" he

asked. He was a little surprised. Usually, Henry didn't talk seriously. But something seemed to be troubling him.

"Oh, nothing . . ." he sighed. "I just get lonely sometimes, I suppose." He kept checking over his shoulder for Ava to come out. It was very odd behavior, indeed. "I spend all the winter alone . . . without anyone to watch sunsets with or share a meal with. And . . . well . . . I wanted to tell you . . . before you two go to your home . . . that . . . I really like you a lot . . . and am so grateful to have you as a friend . . . and for all the fun you've given me over the years."

He looked so sad as he spoke, and sounded like it might be the last time they'd see each other.

All kinds of terrible thoughts went through our hero's mind—images of Henry feeling sad and suffering alone in his bear cave. Maybe Henry didn't have enough food to survive in winter this year. Maybe he was sick. Or maybe sick with loneliness. He kept listening.

"Anyways . . ." Henry sighed, drying his tears. "What I am trying to say is . . . I'll miss you." He patted the boy on the head. "You have been like a cub to me."

"You've been a good friend too, Henry," the boy answered. "But we'll see each other again."

"I hope so."

Henry checked over his shoulder again. He saw Ava's shadow in the cave. Soon, she'd be out.

"And what about your dear wolf friend?" Henry asked next. "She is wonderful, isn't she?"

"Yeah, she's great."

"She loves you so much. So much, in fact, I think she would even die for you. Wouldn't you agree?"

"Yeah," answered the boy sadly. "She would. She's the best. Actually she . . ."

The boy paused. Something seemed to be making him sad.

"Yes? What is it, my boy? What's troubling you? Tell me. You can tell your old Uncle Henry."

"Well, it's just . . . she did almost die last winter . . . just like you said."

"Really? Oh, how terrible! I had no idea. What happened?"

"Well," he said gulping, holding back his tears, "I keep getting bigger, you see."

"Yes, I see that. Heh . . . Heh . . ."

"And so, I keep needing more food. I wish I didn't but—well, last year we didn't have enough. We both got sick. But she got real sick —and almost died."

"Oh!" sighed Henry sensitively. "How awful!

She gave you her portions so you wouldn't starve. How much she must love you."

"Yeah . . . and I'm not sure we'll have enough this year either. Though, I've done my best. I really have."

Ava emerged from the cave and saw them talking.

"Yes, that you have, laddy! You're a good boy." He patted our hero on the head again and wiped his tears for him. "But here she comes. Shh!" he whispered. "Don't worry! Your Uncle Henry will help you out. I've got a little surprise for you. It's just down the hill here. You'll see! But here she comes! Let's just keep this little chat between you and me, shall we?"

The boy nodded.

Henry smiled and turned around.

"Ho there! Ava! Over here! Glad you made it out, old friend! So wonderful to see you!"

Ava looked at them suspiciously, wondering why they were looking at her so fondly all of the sudden.

"What?" she asked, disgusted.

"Yes, me too!" said the boy running up to her. "I'm glad you're here!"

Our hero gave Ava a big hug.

"Ugh—yuck! Get off me!" She pushed him off. "What's gotten into you?"

"Sorry!"

"What were you two talking about?"

"Oh, nothing," answered Henry. "Only that we should get you and our handsome young man here back home as soon as possible."

"Hmph," Ava scoffed. "Well . . . good. Let's go then."

"Yes! Yes! How stupid of me for stalling! Thank you for being so patient with a forgetful old bear like me. Tee! He! He!"

He then whispered to the boy before running on ahead.

"Psst! Follow me! This way! I have a surprise. You have nothing to worry about. Come! Come down here and see for yourself!"

He tickled and pinched himself as he ran and began another song:

> *Friends! Friends!*
> *Helping each other!*
> *Friends! Friends!*
> *I've got one like no other!*
> *I'm gonna surprise my friend!*
> *It's just around the bend!*
> *We just need to descend . . .*
> *A little farther!*

9

HENRY'S SURPRISE

A s I am sure you can tell by now, dear reader, our hero wasn't very bright. It was his one big weakness. Henry the Bear knew this and used it to set a most ingenious trap for him. A trap that would have very painful consequences, but also lead to the beginning of one of the greatest adventures ever told.

It's a very sad part of our story, I'm sorry to have to tell you. It's also, I'm afraid, quite scary. If there was ever a time to skip ahead or hide under the covers, that time would certainly be now. But if you're feeling brave, I would encourage you to read on. Here is what happened to him that day.

After guiding our hero and Ava through the tunnel, Henry led them down into Snake Valley —a dark, barren and dusty wasteland that was famous for its tall, thin mountain in the middle, called Snake Mountain. It was black and jagged looking—like out of a nightmare—and full of little holes where the deadliest snakes lived. At night, you could see their eyes glowing out of the shadows. If it was quiet enough, you could even hear their hisses and whispers.

The snakes guarded a tree at the top that was full of plump, juicy fruit. Many animals in the forest had ventured there and tried to climb for it, but all had failed. Skeletons lay at the bottom and the whole valley was teeming with vultures. They sat in their nests, patiently waiting for whoever would be next. When they saw Henry guiding our hero there, they licked their lips and cackled.

Ava didn't want to be down there at all. She didn't like Snake Valley. Least of all, she cared for surprises. Besides, the first storm of winter was approaching. It was closing in fast. That meant it wasn't long before the winter predators would arrive. The winter predators were stronger than she was and she was afraid that they might even be stronger than our hero. His abilities had not yet been tested against them. All of this made her very nervous.

"Listen," she said. "I don't think we should be here now. Can you please get this over with so we can go home?"

"Relax, Ava," answered Henry. "You'll both

be warm soon enough. I promise! Hee, hee . . ."
He stopped when they got to Snake Mountain.
"Well, here we are! Surprise!"

He directed our hero's attention up to the
fruit at the top. The sunlight glimmered
through it. It looked beautiful—and so delicious. But our hero wasn't excited. If anything,
he just looked sad.

"Hmm? What's wrong?" asked Henry.
"Look! Look! Don't you see it?"

"Yeah, I see it," answered the boy. A cold
shiver went down his spine as he remembered
all his friends who had climbed and fallen.

"You mean, you know about this fruit?"

"Yes," the boy answered, lowering his eyes.
"I'm sorry, Henry. I know you were wanting to
surprise me. But I've been here before. I know
about this place. I have for a long time. But that
fruit is impossible to get. Snakes live there. I've
seen them. They're very dangerous. One bite
can kill. They guard it day and night. Not even
birds will fly up there. It's hopeless. I'm
sorry . . ."

"Yeah," added Ava. "What kind of surprise is
this? We know about this place. Everyone does!
This is what you wanted to show him? Come
on, kid. Let's go. Henry, it was nice knowing
you. Do us a favor now and buzz off."

Ava turned to walk away and signaled the

boy to follow, but Henry wasn't finished with them yet.

"Ho! Ho! Ho!" he laughed, clapping his paws together.

"What?" asked Ava.

"Did you really think that showing you this fruit would be my surprise?"

"Well, you did say 'surprise,' Henry," answered the boy, confused.

"Yes, but it wasn't the FULL surprise. You haven't yet seen that."

"Well get on with it then!" yelled Ava at him. She was getting very impatient with all his games. "We don't have all day!"

"Patience, my friends! Patience!" he chuckled. "It will happen any moment now."

Our hero was intrigued. What could he possibly be waiting for?

"I discovered it two years ago," Henry continued, "as I was walking in these parts, not too far from here. Walking and singing my favorite song! Ahem! Ahem!

I hear a buzzing!
And buzzing means there's bees.
And if there are bees buzzing!
Then there must be hon-ey.
And if there is honey!
Way up in this tree.

Then that means the honey . . .
Must certainly be for me!

"Gah, hah! Come on! Sing it with me! You know the words!"

But the boy didn't know that song at all, and just looked confused. Ava didn't look like she wanted to sing either. So, he just went back to telling his story.

"Ahem! Well! Anyways! As I was saying . . . after I—ugh—asked for the honey very politely, the bees were generous enough to give me some. I took it to this spot so I could sit and eat it. I looked up and saw the fruit! Oh, how delicious it looked! Perfect for winter! See how it glows! But, drat! So high up! Too high! And so very dangerous to climb too! Especially at my time of life! I almost left at that moment. It seemed like an impossible task, as you said. But then—and I don't know what it was—something inside me told me to wait just a little longer. So, I did. And that's when it happened!"

Henry started wagging his stubby little tale as he recalled it. Our hero's eyes lit up curiously.

"What, Henry? You saw what?"

"Well, take a look, my boy! And see for yourself!"

Our hero and Ava looked at each other confused, and shrugged. Neither of them saw anything out of the ordinary. Snake Mountain seemed as it always was—barren and dry. But then, suddenly, a cold gust of wind swooshed down into the valley from the approaching storm. A wind so strong that it frightened the vultures and even toppled a few of their nests. They all began cackling and fleeing. Then the wind hit Snake Mountain. You could hear it whistle as it passed through the little holes. That's when our hero and Ava saw what Henry was talking about.

Terrified and frozen, all of the snakes suddenly slithered out of the mountain. They came out and down the slope. They raced right past our heroes and Henry, and down into the ground wherever there were open spaces. It wasn't long until Snake Mountain appeared entirely empty. But the fruit in the tree near the top was still intact. Our hero and Ava were left utterly astonished.

"Hah, hah!" laughed Henry. He began dancing and prancing around, tickling and pinching himself more. "Ooh hoo hoo! Hee hee! Look! Look! It worked! It happened again! I knew it! I knew it! Look! Snake Mountain is empty!"

"Wow . . ." gasped the boy in amazement. "Yeah, you're right. It sure looks like it."

At first, Ava thought it was just a stupid

trick that only two stupid animals like Henry and our hero could possibly be amused by. But then she started to realize what Henry was doing—and became very upset.

"Hey! Wait a minute! This is your big surprise? You want to climb up there?"

"What? Me! Hah!" Henry cackled. "You must be joking. Look at me! I could never get up there. My paws are too big to grip the holes. And at my time of life!?"

"Oh, so you want him to go and get it for you then? Is that it?"

"I never said that," answered Henry. "But now that you mention it, it does sound like an interesting idea . . . doesn't it, sonny?"

"Oh, please. You expect us to believe that? No—you planned this whole thing out, didn't you? Let me guess. You didn't prepare for winter. You want us to do your work for you. Well, you can forget it."

"Ava," sighed Henry, offended. "I would never ask either of you to do a thing like that for me. I brought you here so that you two could have it, not me."

"Why!?"

"Why? Well, because you're my friends! Right, bucko?" he said, turning to the boy. Our hero agreed.

"I don't believe it!" answered Ava. "A bear

dragging someone all the way out here just to be generous? No, you're up to something! I know it!"

Henry crossed his arms and looked very hurt by her words.

"Besides," Ava continued, "even if he were to climb up there—how is he supposed to get it down? Did *that* thought ever cross your brain?"

"Now, now, Ava," chuckled Henry. "Look, I wouldn't expect you to understand. But some of us like helping others. Don't we, my boy?" Our hero nodded. "And, of course, I've thought of that! How would he get it down? What a silly question! Why don't you open your eyes and see? Look! Right over here!"

Henry strutted over to a small, but deep pool of water that was located beneath where the fruit hung. He dipped his paw in and splashed them with it just to make sure they knew he wasn't lying.

"Hah! You see, laddy? You can drop it right in here. The water will break its fall. Easy!"

The boy ran over and inspected it for himself. It was indeed under the fruit. It seemed wide and deep enough. Everything checked out.

"It's perfect!" he yelled out. "You know what? I think it could actually work!"

"Exactly! You see? Your old Uncle Henry came through, just like he said!"

Henry messed up his hair and splashed him some more. Our hero laughed wildly and then threw himself into the bear's arms, giving him a big hug.

"Oh, Henry! Thank you! I love the surprise! You're so smart! You're the best bear in the world! Thank you! I love you!"

For a moment, Henry felt a little guilty, reader. His plan was working perfectly. As bad as a bear as he was, there was something about the boy that sometimes made him feel warm and fuzzy. He didn't like the feeling. But he had to pretend to.

"Aww . . ." he finally said. "Thank you . . ." He patted our hero on the head and proceeded to pry him off. "But you'd better hurry. Look! It's growing colder every minute! Winter is coming. The edges of the pond are beginning to freeze. You don't have much time. If you wait any longer, whatever falls here will be squashed —and become a frozen jelly popsicle!"

He licked his lips and smiled. Our hero looked over at the approaching storm and agreed. But Ava still wasn't buying it. And she was growing more frustrated.

"No!" she barked and growled. "You mustn't do this! The storm is too close. Even if you managed to get to the top, and even if there are no snakes left, there is no time! It's too dangerous. We're running late as it is! I can't believe how foolish you two are. You're so—"

But as Ava became enraged and began to scold him, as Henry predicted she would, the clever bear put his paw on the boy's shoulder and began whispering.

"Aww . . . Ava really does care about you, doesn't she? Look at how protective she is. I think that's what I would miss most about her, wouldn't you?"

This caught our hero's attention and made him completely stop listening to whatever Ava was saying.

"Yeah . . ." he nodded sadly.

Henry frowned and continued.

"Oh, I can't bear the thought of Ava starving again. The illness it caused. Then you would be alone. I'm sure you can imagine what that might be like. Have you thought about it sometimes? Being alone?" The boy nodded again and lowered his eyes. "Yes, I thought so. Me too. Wouldn't feel very good knowing you could have prevented it, either."

"No . . ." our hero squeaked.

Ava just kept ranting angrily, not noticing what Henry was doing.

"But you can," whispered Henry. "I know you want to. Because you're such a good, good boy. You don't want to be responsible for anyone dying, do you?"

"No . . ."

"Especially a slow and painful death. This is your friend!"

"Yeah . . ."

Tears were starting to form in his eyes.

"Well," sighed Henry. "Then I think you know what you have to do. Climb it, son. Don't let her die like this! Save her! Choose life! It's in your power. I've seen you climb. You're SO good at it. You can do it! I know you can. It will only take a minute if you hurry. But you mustn't delay any longer. Please . . . I beg you . . . I don't want us to lose her either. Do it for me, too!"

Henry had our hero almost shaking in sadness. He remembered how sick she got last year. He remembered how he felt. He would have done almost anything if he could have.

Ava was midway through her lecture about the danger before she noticed Henry had been talking to him. She became even angrier.

"Hey! Wait a minute! What are you!—" Until she saw the boy's expression.

He had the same look he did last year in the cave. She knew instantly what Henry must have been whispering to him. She also realized that getting angry wasn't going to change his mind. Yet, she knew she had to. She walked over. For the very first time in her life, Ava spoke gently to him.

"Don't worry about me, kid . . . I'll be fine. Really."

"That's what you always say," our hero despaired. "But things keep getting worse every year—all because of me."

He hated that he didn't stop growing and always needed more food.

"Everybody dies one day," she answered. "It's just the way it is. We can't change that. And I'm okay with it. Besides, I'm tougher than you think. I don't believe I'll die. I might not even get sick. We've done good this year. I'm a survivor. I'll be fine. And even if I'm not, you will be."

Henry didn't like this at all. He didn't actually expect her to talk to him this way.

"But neither of us will survive if you climb this mountain now," she continued. "It cannot be done. Not yet! Listen, if you really want to that badly, we can come back next year. We can practice. We'll do it right—plan it out and everything. But not like this. Don't listen to him. Trust me and let it go this time. Let's go home."

Henry was so worried she'd spoiled his plan, he was almost ready to charge and attack them right then and there.

"That blasted wolf!" he thought. "I'll kill her for this! I'll tear her limb from limb! We'll do it the old-fashioned way, if that's what you want!"

But he did not show it. For the boy still didn't seem like he had decided either way.

The boy looked at the storm. It was getting close. He looked at Ava. She looked like she wanted to go home. She wasn't even mad at him anymore. He looked at Henry, who did his best to smile. Then, he cast his eyes down. He was out of time. He had to choose. So, he thought—which is something, as you know, he really wasn't good at—and he made a very, very silly decision.

"I'm sorry, Ava. I . . . can't . . . I just can't bear the thought of losing you because of me—because I was too scared. I'm sorry. But don't worry. I'm going to get it. You'll see. I'll climb up and cut it down. We'll have lots to eat this winter. You will be okay. I promise."

And with that, Henry and Ava's feelings switched. Now, she felt like tearing Henry apart, and he felt better again.

"Oh! Good! Good! Good, boy! Yes, you can do it!" he said comforting him.

Our hero was expecting Ava to get angry again. But instead, she just looked heartbroken.

"Fine . . ." she sighed, giving up. She knew there was no stopping him now. If she stalled him any longer, it would only be making it more dangerous for him. "Go . . . if you must. But . . . please . . . please . . . be careful."

Henry couldn't help smiling and giggling. "Don't worry," said our hero. "I'll be up and down in no time!" And he ran off. "Trust me! I'll be right back!"

10

THE FALL

The forest was growing colder every minute. A blanket of snow covered the tree tops. Animals scurried to their burrows and caves, and some fled the forest altogether. Those who weren't prepared either froze or were buried. The wind howled.

Our hero heard all of this, but it did not scare him. He felt the cold air run up his spine, but he did not flinch or shiver. He thought of only one thing: getting up Snake Mountain to get the fruit, so he could save his beloved friend from starvation. With that in mind, he started to climb.

"You know," remarked Henry to Ava, as the boy began his ascent, "I never did understand why you, of all animals, get so ill in winter. You're a wolf. You can go out and find food for yourself. There's plenty to eat—rabbits, foxes, squirrels. All your favorites!"

"I don't eat those," Ava replied. "Not anymore."

"Oh, yes . . . that's right. You've changed. You no longer eat any of the nice little creatures. But there are others. Lynxes . . . the polar bears . . . and—"

"I know that."

But the problem was Ava couldn't handle them one on one. She wasn't even sure she could with his help. The boy was strong. But he was slow and clumsy in the snow. He was not yet fully grown. He had not yet mastered all of the elements. And without a pack, and considering how much slower wounds heal in winter, it was all too dangerous for Ava. It was best just to wait.

"Ah, that's right. I forgot . . . you'd be alone! That's the other thing I've often wondered. Do you sometimes miss being in a pack?"

"No," replied Ava sternly.

"You were certainly in quite the powerful one, I must say. Maul's gang—am I right?"

Ava didn't answer.

"In fact, I've heard you were quite the ranking officer! Ho! Ho! Ho! And even more than that. I heard you two were once—"

"Would you be quiet already! Can't you see I'm trying to watch! Buzz off!"

She ran ahead to get a closer look. Henry followed her, wagging his little tail.

Our hero had only been climbing for a couple of minutes before he realized he was carrying far more weight than he needed. So, he dropped his staff, shield and bow and arrows. Then, he dropped his green armor. It all crashed to the ground.

"There, that's better," he said.

The holes in the mountain fit his hands and feet perfectly. It was simply a matter of finding the fastest way up. For there were some areas with more holes than others and some patches with no place to grasp at all. He soon discovered there were also some old roots that grew down the side. If he reached one, he could use it like a rope and cover a lot of distance. He tried to reach those whenever he could. Though, he had to be careful. Some were rotten and would snap! He had a few close calls that made Ava very, very nervous as she watched.

"Wow! He's going pretty fast!" laughed Henry. "Faster than I expected! He's already halfway up! You've trained him well. You should be proud!"

"I told you to be quiet! I'm not interested in talking to you, okay? Just leave me—"

But then something caught Ava's attention. "What? Oh no!" And she started running towards the mountain, barking. "Hey! Hey! Look out! Look out!"

Our hero only heard it faintly.

"Hmm . . . that's strange," he said. "Ava never barks—unless there's trouble. Is she okay?"

He looked down and saw her running around frantically.

"Ava! What is it?" he yelled down. "Is something wrong? Hey, look how far I've climbed! I'm doing good! I'm alright, see?"

Henry was enjoying all of this. He broke into laughter. Then, Ava got the idea to run fast in the direction she wanted him to look. Finally, it worked. He turned his head toward the storm. And when he looked, he saw and understood why she was in such a frenzy.

"Ahh!" he yelled. Suddenly, out of nowhere, another storm cloud had formed. It was halfway between him and the greater storm that was already coming. And that meant he had only half the time he previously thought. "Wow! No way! Where did THAT come from!?"

As far as Ava was concerned, it was over. There was no way he could make it up and down in time now. It was moving fast and even more violently. It looked like a tornado. His only option was to give up.

"You can do it, laddy!" called out Henry instead. "I believe in you! You can do it! Climb! Hurry! You must go fast! Look! You're already half way!"

"Would you shut up!" growled Ava. "What are you trying to do? Look! It's over! Stop encouraging him!"

Henry just laughed.

"Brah! Hah! Hah! Muah, hah, hah, hah, hah!"

Our hero had to make a decision. He thought and thought. He used his brain. He looked up. He looked down. He looked back up again. He looked back down. He looked at his fingers, trying to calculate whether he had enough time. He thought so hard. But he couldn't do the math.

"Ugh . . . hmm . . . let's see here . . . hmm . . . umm . . . Ah, whatever!" he finally decided. "I'm going to keep going! I can do it! I know I can. I must!"

Henry saw him begin climbing again and started dancing around to celebrate, wagging his behind and cheering.

"Ooh! Hoo! Hoo! Haw, haw! Ho! Ho! Ho!"

Ava would have attacked him if she wasn't so worried about her friend.

"I can do it . . ." the boy repeated to himself. "I can do it . . ." He kept going faster and faster, thinking of how good it would feel to finally reach the top! The proud look on Ava's face as he got it down! "I can do it! Just a little further. I'm almost there!"

As the storm cloud got closer, however, the air grew much colder. Our hero's fingers numbed. His joints stiffened. He became slower and struggled to grip the rock. Then the snow came. It whipped against his skin. Some of it melted—and then froze. A layer of ice began to form over him, just as it was forming over the pond below. It got into his eyes and caused his lids to stick. He constantly had to wipe them. He had not thought it was going to be this bad.

Soon, the cloud began to surround him. He couldn't see the bottom anymore. Neither could Ava or Henry see him. The only light now came from the flashes as the storm intensified. The thunder and howling of the wind deafened him. It sounded, reader, like a train grinding and screeching on tracks—and coming straight towards him! Before long, he couldn't see anything —not even the fruit. But he knew he was getting close.

From down below, it looked like a tidal wave in the sky crashing against the shore. And still, the worst of it hadn't reached him.

The point soon came when our hero couldn't climb any longer. He was too cold. It was so windy he knew he would be blown off if he dared move one of his hands or feet. But he could feel the storm getting worse. He knew that, soon, he was going to get blown off anyways. So, he took his chances and, with all of his might, threw himself up, hoping there would be something, anything he could hold onto. In mid jump, he nearly got sucked away! But, somehow, by some blind stroke of luck, his hand caught the branch of the fruit tree.

He was now flailing like a flag on a pole, no idea whether he was being blown up, down or sideways. He knew only that he had made it. He was almost there!

"Come on . . ." he moaned. "Don't give up now!"

Lightning struck next to our hero. He flinched and almost let go. With every ounce of remaining strength he had left, he pulled himself up through the torrent, got a leg up and wrapped himself around the branch.

It was so loud he couldn't hear his own cries —or even his thoughts. Nor could he breathe. The storm sucked away the air in front of him. Sometimes right out of his lungs. All he could do was hang on now. There was nowhere left to go.

The last thing he remembered was looking up at the fruit on the tree. It was plump, bright and red—half-covered in snow. But behind the fruit, where the wind was blowing from, was darkness. He saw the snow blowing in his face. He saw the black center coming towards him. Lightning flared all around it. It kept getting closer and colder and louder. He longed to cover his ears for fear his head would explode—but how could he let go of the branch? Then he saw a bright light.

A moment later, the branch he was on snapped! With our hero half-conscious, wrapped around the trunk, the branch launched from the cloud like a cannon. The whole thing was on fire. It skipped down the mountain-side, slamming into the rock over and over. Finally, it plunged through the pond and shattered the ice —along with most of our hero's bones.

11

HENRY CHANGES

Our hero awoke under freezing cold water, unable to move. He didn't remember how he got there or even whether he was dreaming. All he knew was that he couldn't breathe—and he began to panic.

Fortunately, Ava found him just in time. She dove in and pulled him out onto the snow. He coughed up water. It froze as soon as it hit the air. That's when the pain returned. All at once, every bone in his body felt like it was on fire. He cried out in agony.

"Quiet!" growled Ava. She was relieved he was alive, but terrified he would attract more danger. Winter's predators always accompanied the first storm. They needed to get out of there as soon as possible. She could check on him later. "Can you stand?"

Our hero could not. He couldn't even move —but only whimper.

"Agh! Ava . . ."

He started tugging on her fur with the only arm that worked.

"What?" she asked coldly.

"I'm . . . I'm sorry . . ."

"Never mind that, now. Just keep quiet. We'll have to carry you." She kept looking over her shoulder and sniffing the air.

"O . . . okay . . ." the boy squeaked.

"Henry, come and give me a hand," Ava called out. But there was no answer. "Henry?" She looked around for him. He was standing in the snow, not moving, not talking, not even blinking. No expression on his face either. He just stood there, staring.

"H-h-Henry . . ." the boy whimpered. "I'm sorry. I couldn't . . . get it. P-please . . . help me . . ."

But he still wasn't responding. It made Ava very nervous. She knew that look in his eye. She'd seen it in animals before. Finally, after it became perfectly clear our hero wasn't getting back up, he spoke. His voice sounded very different from before—lower and more serious.

"Step aside, Ava. You know the rules. Look at him. He's useless. He can no longer serve any purpose."

Our hero didn't understand, but Ava did.

"He's fine! He's just hurt, that's all."

"Gah hah! Just hurt? Please! Look at him! He won't last the night—and you know it."

The boy couldn't believe what he was hearing.

"Henry . . ." he whimpered. "W-what are you saying? We're friends!"

"Friends? Friends? No, child. I don't have any friends."

"But . . . you said . . . you told me . . . and what about—"

"But nothing! I tricked you! Get it? I pretended to be your friend. Those were all lies! I just wanted to eat you! That's why I brought you here. Gah hah! I knew you'd be dumb and desperate enough to climb! I knew you'd fall. And now, you're mine!"

You could almost hear our hero's heart break in two. His eyes filled with tears. The pain was even worse than his broken bones.

"No!" growled Ava. "Over my dead body."

"But I want him."

"Well, you can't have him."

"Why?"

"Because I won't let you."

"Why!?"

"Because—he's too important."

"WHY?"

"I don't know why!" said Ava. "I just know he is and that's enough. You can't have him. Not him. And if you do try, you'll have to go through me."

"Fine," snarled Henry. "Let us settle it the old way. By the ancient law of combat, I will claim him."

He lifted his massive paw and drew out his claws. They were like a set of razor-sharp hooks. He smiled with all of his teeth. Ava bared hers as well. Her hackles shot up. She bent low, ready to charge. Henry charged first.

"Grawr!" he shouted, like a battle cry. He began snorting and squealing like a pig with each stride. *Snort, snort, snort! Wee! Wee!* Then, he bellowed and roared like a bull. *Moo!*

Ava ducked under his paw as he swiped at her. It would have taken her head clean off. She bit into his side, tearing out a chunk of his flesh.

"Agh!" he cried. "Why, you little!" And he used his other paw to backhand her across the jaw. She flew into the snow. Ava felt dizzy after that, and before she could get up, Henry charged again. He headbutted her this time. She flew through the air and landed in the pond, the same pond she pulled our hero from. Henry laughed evilly and snorted some more.

"Brah! Hah! Hah! *Snort, snort, snort.* Where are you? *Snort, snort.*" Henry went to the pond and found her. He sunk his claws into her and pulled her out. "Ah! Hah! Gotcha! Heh! Heh! Heh!"

He held her up thinking she was defeated. But she suddenly squirmed free enough to slash him across his left eye. Henry wailed and howled in pain. But it wasn't enough to make him let go. He still held Ava in his clutches—and now he was angry.

"Agh! My eye! So, you want to fight dirty, huh?"

He dunked her back under the water and held her there.

"Thought that was pretty funny, didn't yeh!" he growled.

Our hero saw his friend flapping and struggling. Henry was drowning her. The boy knew she didn't have much time. Henry started laughing again.

"Brah! Hah, hah, hah! Look at her squirm! Having fun under there? Hee, hee, hee!"

The boy looked around. What could he do? That's when he saw his pointed staff. It wasn't far. Maybe he could use his one good arm to crawl and get it. Maybe he could stick Henry with it when he wasn't looking. He tried. He slowly crawled. It was very painful and he knew he couldn't make any sound or Henry would hear.

"Die! Die!" Henry cried out. "Muah! Hah! Hah! Hah!"

Sometimes he would pull her out and give her a quick breath. But it was only because he wanted more time to enjoy drowning her. "Ho! Ho! Ho!"

Finally, our hero made it to his staff. But he couldn't stand up. Even holding it hurt. Still, he knew he had to save his friend. So, with all of his remaining strength, he turned himself onto his back and launched his staff like a javelin. He could feel his broken bones move and the cuts on his body open up more. It hit Henry, but it wasn't very strong or accurate. It merely pricked him in the hip. Nevertheless, it distracted him enough to save Ava.

"Agh!" Henry yelped. He spun around with fury in his eyes and looked at the boy like he was going to charge him next. He lifted Ava out and slammed her on the ground.

"Now," he growled. She couldn't move. "I want you to watch this, Ava. I want you to see me eat him. I want you to hear his cries and begging. I'll start with his toes. Then his legs! Then his knees! His fat little belly! And last, his face!"

Henry looked thoroughly like a monster now. He licked his lips and began kicking his back leg like a bull ready to charge. He let out a bellow. Our hero was frozen in fear. Then Henry ran at him—snorting and oinking like a pig again. *Snort, snort, snort. Wee! Wee! Moo!* Ava was down. Our hero had no more defenses. He was helpless. *Wee! Wee! Snort, snort, snort!* Henry ran right on top of the boy and then stood up on both his hind legs, like a giant. He looked down and roared at him. The sound reminded the boy of being up in the storm. It was over. He knew it. He closed his eyes and braced himself for his doom. But just before Henry struck, he heard a sound in the distance . . .

It was howling. Not Ava's howling. Ava couldn't howl like that. This was something different. Henry recognized it. It was . . . the one in the forest everyone feared—even our heroes: Maul, the winter wolf lord! He was coming with his pack! Henry suddenly went from looking like a monster, to a frightened and cornered mouse. He crouched down and listened again, unsure if it was real or just the wind. "No . . . no . . ." he stuttered. Then he heard it again. All three of them did. *Owooo!*

Maul was no ordinary wolf. He was three times bigger, pure muscle, with massive razor-sharp fangs. He was known for singlehandedly slaying animals as big as elephants. He only came in winter. The fact that he had come this early meant he must have been extra hungry.

Henry had almost forgotten the boy was still there. He sniffed the air and looked around wildly. He started shaking.

"Oh, no . . . he's here."

He glanced down at our hero and Ava and put his claws away. He wanted to eat them, but he dared not stay a moment longer. He left them in the snow and took off running. The boy never saw him in that forest again.

Our hero sunk into the snow, exhausted. Ava struggled to her feet and limped over to check on him.

"He's gone," she said. "Good riddance."

The boy was sprawled out, almost buried. The blizzard was getting heavier. It was a sad sight to behold. He was helpless. It reminded Ava of when she first found him in the snow as a baby.

"Now," she said. "Listen! You've got to get up now. We've got to go. Henry is gone. But Maul will be here soon. He's a thousand times worse. I can't take him by myself. His pack will track us down and find us. You've got to get up."

"I can't, Ava," our hero whined. "Look at me. I can't get up. Just leave me. I don't mind. Like you said, everybody dies."

"Enough of that!" she barked. "Move it, I said! I never asked for your opinion! On your feet, soldier! Now!"

"Ugh . . .okay . . ." he squeaked. "I'll . . . try."

"That's it!"

He attempted to use his good arm to lift himself up. He pushed with all his strength, but he just collapsed. Then they heard more howls. It was much louder and clearer. They were getting close. Ava sensed this right away and she lost all patience.

"Grr! Get up!" she barked, as though trying to scare him now—as though she was going to eat him herself if he didn't obey. "GET UP! GET UP! GET UP! NOW!"

He tried again—but failed. He fell even harder and it hurt even more. Now he was screaming in pain. Maul would hear them for sure! They were probably already bounding toward them, closing in.

"I can't!" our hero cried. "I can't . . . I'm sorry!"

"Blast!" said Ava. "Fine. Have it your way. I'll carry you myself." She got down, bit into his arm and threw him over her shoulder, onto her back. "Hold on," she commanded him. "And bite down on my fur if you need to. This is going to hurt—a lot. And you're going to need to be quiet. No more of this whining." And she took off at full speed.

Ava hurried with him through the rest of Snake Valley and into another part of the forest.

She could hear and even smell the other wolves behind her. They were hungry. They were growling. Maul himself wouldn't have been far behind. She weaved through the trees. She knew these woods well—including the places where her and the boy had placed traps. For they were now getting very close to their cave. She was heading to their secret back entrance.

Ava could hear the twigs they laid snap and the yelps as Maul's minions fell into the holes they'd dug. A few got close. The boy could feel their breath on his feet as they nipped at his heels and toes. Ava kicked them away.

She outsmarted them with shortcuts and led some into traps. Four wolves got caught in a big net. Two were crushed under a log that fell from the trees. One was shot with an arrow from a bow that had been placed in a bush. But there were still a lot more of the gang coming.

Finally, Ava reached the entrance. She hit a switch the boy had designed that released large stones to block the way in. The other wolves nearly made it inside with them, but were crushed. *Boom! Boom! Boom!* It sounded like bowling balls being dumped down a flight of stairs. Our heroes barely avoided being crushed themselves. But they had made it.

THE CAVE

Ava hauled our hero through over three miles of darkness before arriving at their lair. She dropped him. He was too out of breath to cry and in too much pain to faint. All he could do was lay there wild-eyed, wheezing and quivering.

It was a simple cave. There was one room, four stone walls and a low ceiling. But it was also very colorful. Each wall was covered with paintings. Some were of himself and Ava. Others were of trees, flowers or other things he liked. But most of them were pictures of inventions he designed, like new weapons, traps or gliders. Beneath were scattered tools, parts and all the failed attempts to build them. There was a corner in his cave for food and another for wood. Near the front and back entrances were racks of various weapons. The fire pit was in the middle, next to where he slept.

Ava sniffed around the cave and inspected the front entrance to make sure there were no intruders. She went outside, where there was a little terrace that overlooked the great valley. Their cave was on the side of a mountain. All the paths up to the terrace were blocked or booby-trapped and the ice building up at the bottom would make it very difficult for anyone to climb. For now, they were safe.

Ava descended again and went over to the wood pile. She put a few logs together then brought over some flint. That's a special kind of rock for lighting fires.

"Here," she said, handing it to him.

With his one working arm and the very last of his strength, he reached out and struck it against another rock to make a spark. He felt some more of the broken bones in his body shift as he did so, but still didn't have enough breath to cry out. Instead, he just collapsed again. He wouldn't be moving anymore that night.

The spark caught fire. Ava shuffled it closer to him and examined his wounds. It was bad. Very bad. Both his legs were broken in different spots. One arm was broken. He had deep gashes, scrapes and burns. But she didn't say anything. Then, she went to their food pile and brought over his favorite dish. A big smelly fish with some strawberry jam.

"Eat," she said coldly. "You'll need your strength."

"S-s-strength?" muttered the boy. "F-f-for what?"

"For the pain. I need to straighten you out and clean your wounds. It's going to hurt."

Our hero chuckled. Or was he crying? Ava couldn't tell. It was going to hurt? More pain? What did that even mean? He felt like he was already in as much pain as possible.

"Eat!" Ava insisted, this time with a growl. But our hero refused.

"No!" He looked at her with fury and defiance in his eyes. "Leave me . . . alone."

Ava glared at him. He glared right back. Then finally, she gave in.

"Fine," she said. "Well . . . aren't we grouchy today?" She turned around and put the food back onto the pile. "But I guess I shouldn't be surprised. You've always been a picky eater, ever since you were a baby. A spoiled little brat. Always whining and complaining. Nothing was ever good enough for you. Even though I brought you nothing but the best gourmet meals."

"Oh, please," groaned the boy. "Gourmet

meals? You brought me chewed up worms and slugs! I hated that gruel! Ouch!"

It hurt to talk, but Ava knew she had to do something to keep his mind off the pain, or he'd faint and never wake up. Even worse, he looked like he wouldn't have minded. She had to keep him attentive and alert.

"Any wolf cub would have been happy to get such a meal."

"Well, fine—but I wasn't a wolf!"

"Indeed. You were a frail, little, ugly weakling—bald and babbling. I was so disappointed. How in the world was I going to turn something so pathetic and useless into a soldier?"

"You could have started by protecting me! I was only a baby. The bugs . . . I remember you sitting there, doing nothing, letting them eat me."

"You deserved it," replied Ava. "Served you right for letting them. Besides, you needed to learn. Life is war. And you did learn." Then Ava's eyes started to light up and she smiled. "Ah, yes! I still remember it! You made your first tiny little fist. You slammed it into them, one by one. Crushed your enemies! Crawled all around the cave! Destroyed them utterly!" Ava almost had tears in her eyes as she recalled it. "Your first genocide . . . I was so proud . . ."

"You're . . . insane . . ." answered the boy. He looked away and closed his eyes like he didn't want to talk about it anymore.

"Well," said Ava. "You say that now. But there is a method to my madness. You have to admit—it came in handy the time the bat attacked you."

This got his attention again. He looked up at Ava surprised.

"What? The bat? You were there . . . when the bat attacked me?" Ava smiled and nodded at him. "But it almost killed me. You were there? Watching? As that THING tried to eat me alive!?"

Though our hero was only about one year old at the time, he remembered it like it was yesterday. He had exterminated and consumed all the bugs he could find in the cave and felt like he could finally get a good night's sleep. He found some comfortable mud to lie in. But in the middle of the night, he felt something sniffing and licking behind his ear. He thought it was the big furry creature. That was what he called Ava. But when he reached beside himself to touch the phantom, he felt leathery skin . . . a fuzzy belly . . . and a little crinkly face . . . with two sharp fangs. It squealed at him as it attacked.

"Ahh!" he remembered screaming. "Help! Help!" These were our hero's first words. "Help! Help! Helllp!" But none answered.

"I can't believe it," said the boy. "I thought you were away at the time. You were THERE? And you did NOTHING!?"

"Why would I? I was testing you."

"A test?"

"Yes. I wanted to see how you'd react when faced with an opponent your own size. Would you curl up into a ball, and let yourself be destroyed—or fight? And I wasn't disappointed. It had you on your back. You were losing! But then I saw the anger build up. Oh, you had a rage inside you, boy. You grabbed that bat by his two big stupid ears and pushed him off. Then you got on top of him and gave him a taste of his own medicine. You made your little fist again and bashed his brains in with it! And then you ate his brains! Slurped em right up!" Ava made a slurp sound as she told the story, making our hero cringe. "Then you tore him to pieces and found his heart. You ate it whole. It was . . . magnificent. And the bats never bothered you again after that, did they?"

"No."

"It's then I knew you had real potential. But there was still one last test."

"The climb," the boy muttered, re-membering.

"Yes."

Our hero endured many months in the cave, surrounded by darkness, freezing temperatures and the worst imaginable smells. His baby food was vomit, worms and bugs—all of which made him ill. The air felt poisonous. He was always coughing and his skin was bumpy and itchy from getting bitten.

Eventually, he started exploring. He felt his way along the cave floor. He found rocks, bones and soon the stone walls of the cave.

He discovered two special walls as well. One was black and the other was white. The black wall frightened him. It was colder and quieter. He heard bats there—flapping, squeaking and giggling.

"Join us . . ." they whispered to him.

"Come down and play . . . Tee hee!"

He scurried away and never went near it again.

But the white wall was different. It was warm and pretty. The air nearby was fresher. It sent down all kinds of curious echoes and shad-ows. Sounds and shapes of things he'd never seen or heard before. It made him curious and want to approach. But it was at the top of a path too steep to climb. Every time he tried, he fell and hurt himself.

"It didn't occur to you to help at all?" our hero answered as Ava cleaned his wounds. "Agh! Ouch! Ouch!" It was working. The talk was keeping him awake and distracted. But she still needed more time.

"No, it didn't," she continued. "As I said, you needed to learn. There is no 'help' out here. You needed to learn to help yourself. And if you couldn't help yourself—because you were too weak—then you needed to learn to become strong. And you did learn this, too—when the pain eventually became unbearable."

Our hero remembered it well. Life got even harder for him down there. Much of it was because there weren't any diapers or bathrooms. As you can imagine, it started smelling very bad very quickly and began attracting swarms of new bugs. They joined forces and waged constant, perpetual war upon him. The only way he survived was to cover himself in thick oozing mud.

This was also when the nightmares started to come. Our hero began having horrifying dreams about being a bat. His face would be crinkly! He'd have pointed ears, leathery skin and fangs! All day long, he'd hang upside down at the black wall, squeaking! He would wake up in a panic and check himself to make sure it wasn't real. But that was the scariest part of all. He couldn't check! It was too dark to see. There were no mirrors. He couldn't even feel his own skin anymore. Maybe it was true. Maybe he was a bat—or becoming one. The thought of it tormented him just as much as their taunting.

"Join us! Join us!"

"It's fun being a bat! *Squeak, squeak*!"

He felt like he was starting to go mad. Eventually, he snapped—just as Ava had predicted.

"No!" he cried. This was his second word. He wasn't going to become one of those things! Nor was he going to become bug food! He had to get to the white wall somehow. He sat up and tore the mud off himself.

"Ah, pain!" sighed Ava, remembering. "Nature's greatest teacher! Finally, you realized what you needed to do."

Day and night, our hero crawled as fast as he could around the cave. He crawled back and forth. He crawled in circles. He crawled up on top of things. Even when he skinned his hands and knees and was bleeding all over the floor! It didn't matter. Nor did it matter how terrible his food tasted anymore. If insects and gruel gave him energy and made him grow, then that's what he needed to eat. He began stuffing himself with the biggest, juiciest bugs and worms he could find. Even big, hairy spiders! He would throw it all up, of course. But even that didn't stop him. He'd pool it together with his hands and then slurp it up from the floor! He was that desperate to get strong. And it made Ava very proud to watch.

"That isn't all I learned," said the boy, trying not to look as Ava straightened out his bones. "Agh! Ouch!"

"No?"

"No. I learned that the white wall . . . couldn't have been a wall. It was . . . something else—a door."

"How did you figure that out? You had never seen it up close yet."

"I just knew it," he answered. "It was the only thing that made any sense. Why else would I have been so miserable down there? I had desires for things too—things that weren't in the cave. Why would they be in me? Why was it that, when I smelled the air from the white wall, my mouth watered? There had to have been food. And if there was food, then it was a place."

The fateful day finally arrived.

"I remember it was storming," our hero recalled. Ava remembered it too. It was the first thunderstorm of spring. "I was scared."

Flashes lit up the cave as if the white wall was angry. Thunder shook the ground like an earthquake. Parts of the ceiling began to crack and crumble. Water poured in like a rushing river, causing a great flood. He had to climb up onto a rock just to keep himself from being washed away—washed down to the black wall where the bats were! The big furry creature got up and began its ascent towards the light, leaving him behind. Now! Now was the time!

Our hero leaped and plunged into the roaring waters. He couldn't swim. And in some parts, when the water had mixed with the mud, it felt like quicksand pulling him down. But it didn't stop him. He paddled! He willed himself through, all the way, until he got to the foot of the path. He reached and stretched up with his little arms, just like he'd been practicing, dug his fingers into the mud, and hauled himself up using one arm at a time.

It didn't matter that he was sinking or sliding, how blinding the white wall was the closer he got, or that worms were getting in his mouth and bugs in his teeth. It didn't matter that he lost all of his finger nails from having to dig them into the rocks. He wasn't going to stay there any longer! He'd either ascend or be buried trying. Anything but that place. Just thinking of it made him angry. It gave him extra strength during the moments when he would have ordinarily given up. Finally, he reached the top! Emerged victorious! Breathing his first breath of fresh air!

He arrived just as the storm was dispersing and the sun was coming out. The light of it dazzled his senses. He lost his balance and tumbled forth out of the cave entrance onto the grassy terrace.

His eyes were open, but he couldn't see. The light was blinding. He could feel it burning through his eyeballs and brain. But it wasn't a bad pain. It was a good kind. The kind of pain like when our foot falls asleep, and then slowly starts to wake up. That's how his whole head was feeling. And eventually, he did begin to see.

First, he saw the shadows. For he had seen those before in the cave. His eyes were already well-adjusted to them. Then, he saw something new: colors! Greens! Blues! Reds! Next, he saw reflections. He felt a puddle in front of him. He dunked his head in and washed off the mud. He looked at it and saw himself. He wasn't a bat! He was a—well, he didn't know. But he wasn't a bat! And that was very good news. Then, he looked up and saw the whole valley in all its beauty and splendor.

But one thing caught his attention more than anything else. Something bright red and sweet-smelling! It was a big plump strawberry on a little bush. He crawled over and plucked it. He put it in his mouth and bit down, tasting all the sweet juices. Now, his mouth felt like it was waking up! It overwhelmed him and tears of joy began streaming down his face, a feeling he had never felt before. And for the very first time, our hero smiled.

"You are a very odd creature, aren't you?" said Ava to him then, as she was watching. Those were her first words to him. The boy heard her voice and looked up. So, that's what the big furry creature looked like. He stared at her in amazement and smiled even bigger, his face covered with red mush. "But you know, this isn't the end. It is only the beginning. You are destined to become a soldier." Our hero had no idea what she was talking about at that age. But he liked the sound of her voice. "Enjoy your strawberries, little one. Rejoice. You have earned them." Then, she walked away to leave him alone more. Just don't get too comfortable. Your training starts tomorrow. That's when the real pain begins."

Our hero sat there all afternoon, admiring the view. But he wondered where the white door had gone. He looked around for it. Finally, he turned his eyes up. What he saw startled him so much that he dropped his strawberries. There was that burning feeling again! He had to use his hands to block it this time. What was the white door doing up there? Our hero then learned that he'd been mistaken once again. It wasn't a door. It wasn't a wall. It was what he would soon come to call "the sun." And he learned it was a very special thing, too! For not only was it a thing he saw, but the thing by which he saw everything else. It was the giver of light and warmth and strawberries—and therefore the best thing of all. He sat staring at it. Then, the moon—and eventually the stars.

The boy was so young then. He only remembered bits and pieces. Recalling that triumphant day used to bring him joy. But now it just made him sad. He was back where he started! Weak! Helpless! Half-blind in the dark and in constant pain.

"Why are you telling me all this?" he asked.

"Because," answered Ava. "You seem to have forgotten."

She finished cleaning and straightening out his wounds.

"I haven't forgotten," said the boy.

"Then why don't you eat anything? Why do you have that look, like you've given up?"

"Because," he answered. "Even if I do survive, what then?"

"What do you mean?"

"I mean—look around! Look at my life . . ."

"What about it? It's a good life. A lot better than most have."

"I know. But that isn't what I—"

"You chose this life. You wanted to be the guardian. That comes with risks. You knew that ever since you started."

"It isn't the fighting I'm talking about. It's after. I like what I do. It's just—something's not right. I don't have a home."

"This is your home."

"No, it isn't. I'm sure of it." Our hero looked around. "I'm not happy here."

"Well, we've searched everywhere else for something better."

"Have we?" our hero asked. "I'm not sure."

He realized that once he started protecting others, he'd stopped looking. But did they really search everywhere? If he desired it, then maybe —just like the strawberry—that was a sign it was still out there somewhere. His imagination started to run wild thinking about what it might be like. Ava noticed such thoughts started bringing color back to his face. His breathing returned to normal. He looked like his old self again. Maybe, she thought, that would be the key to his surviving.

"I'll tell you what," she said. "I'll make you a deal." Our hero looked up at her and listened. "You get through this winter alive and, come this spring, we will embark on a journey to find this place you speak of."

"Really?" The boy's eyes lit up.

Ava nodded.

"Alright," he answered, surprised by the suggestion. His mind started racing again.

"Good. Then you can start with this."

Ava brought over the fish and jam again and dropped it on him. Our hero finally conceded and started eating.

But where would this place be? In what direction? It was nothing but mountains on every side of the valley. If he chose wrongly, they might never find it. He couldn't help feel a little worried.

"Look," said Ava. She caught a glimpse of light from the entrance. "The sunset is coming out. Your favorite. Just in time . . ."

Our hero gazed out of the entrance. The storm was passing. A bright golden light peeked through the clouds and over the horizon.

"Where does it go?" he thought dreamily, just as he had that afternoon on the way back from the Life Tree. "Someplace it's always warm, probably. Someplace it's comfortable. Some-place where there are lots of strawberries—and who knows what else?" Then, it suddenly oc-curred to him. "Wait a minute—of course! The sun! Towards the sun! Over that horizon!" That was where his next adventure lay! That was where he would find his home. Or, if he couldn't, someone who might be able to help him.

THE ADVENTURE CONTINUES IN...

THE ADVENTURES OF PHILIP & SOPHIE

—THE SWORD OF THE DRAGON KING—

PART II

ABOUT THE AUTHOR

Drew Eldridge is a tutor from Winnipeg, Manitoba. He has a Bachelor of Arts Degree, majoring in English from the University of Winnipeg, specializing in Young People's Texts and Cultures.

ACKNOWLEDGMENTS

Thank you to my family and friends for supporting one of my great passions in life. Special thanks to my lovely wife, Loralee Eldridge, for helping with revisions. I would also like to thank Lori Brammall for helping review the first and second drafts.